A GOBLIN POSTMAN GOTHIC MYSTERY

I0654635

STORM

WATCH

PATRICIA BOW

This book is for

all lovers of gothic mystery and romance

no matter what their vintage.

Chapter 1

THE HAND WAS MASCULINE. You could see it in the solid strength of wrist bones, the emphatic knuckles, the fingers that were long and smooth but capable-looking. It was poised in the act of reaching, fingers slightly spread. The very shape of it held purpose.

Cally thought she detected menace in it too. She frowned.

The reaching hand covered the middle half of a large poster taped to the inside of a rain-washed glass door on Dundas Street. Along the upper margin ran the words: TORONTO CENTRAL UNIVERSITY / MFA GRADUATE EXHIBITION 3 of 4. And along the lower margin: REGINE ALAINE / SHEILA FORREST / HECTOR WU / JUNE 29-30. Then the TCU Gallery hours. Closing was at six p.m. It was now five fifty-five. *Made it just in time!*

Cally pushed open the glass door and shut it behind her on the drumming rain. Careful not to splash the biscuit-coloured walls, she hung her raincoat and umbrella on the rack. Then pushed a curtain of straight brown hair back from her damp cheeks, and looked around for Noel or Sheila. They weren't among the few figures still browsing through the pictures in the first room.

Somebody else was standing outside where she had been, in front of the poster, making up his mind whether or not to come in out of the rain, Cally guessed. Probably torn between the claims of art and a nice dry pub.

The rain running down the window reduced everything outside to mysterious blurs of colour. Tossing greenery, smears of moving white and red, and, by the door, a big squared dark shape topped by

1

the sketch of a face. No hat, no umbrella. Apparently he didn't mind getting soaked.

"Cally! We'd just about given up on you!" Noel came forward with both hands held out. She gave him a quick kiss on the cheek.

"Sorry, I was signing up for interviews at a job fair. Think I've got a chance at one: writer for a new tech company — a bunch of bright-eyed boys who can write code but not English, at least not intelligibly."

"Oh-oh! Does this mean–"

"No, I won't let you down! They won't be hiring until the fall."

"Thank heaven! I don't know how we'd cope with Ginny without you!"

Laughter relaxed the lines of Noel's chronically worried face. With those lines he could have been years older than his actual twenty-four, which was also her age, and Sheila's. And with his soft fair hair, fine features and cornflower-blue eyes, he could have been years younger. He held her off at arm's length, then deftly set straight the shoulder seams of her already neat red top. She tolerated this annoying habit for the sake of old acquaintance. Noel himself wore a cream linen suit which looked as if it had never been rained on or sat down in.

"Where's Sheila? I'm all excited to see her show."

"She's in the next room, talking to visitors. Coping quite well, really." He slipped an arm around her shoulders. "This will interest you, for a start. Sheila's work, but not part of her main group. This is where you'll be, day after tomorrow. Like it?"

"This" was a watercolour view of a large, handsome Victorian house, gleaming white against a deep green background. Smaller sketches showed details of wooden gingerbread and trellises burdened with purple clematis.

"Mm. Not your average bush cabin!"

"I'd better get back." Noel's smile didn't quite reach his eyes. "I promised I wouldn't leave her alone too long."

"I'll be right with you." Left on her own, Cally lingered over a second group of watercolours, scenes of Stone Face Island and Lake St. Jude. It would be no hardship at all to spend a few weeks in that idyllic-looking spot, even with Ginevra factored in.

The outside door opened, letting in a flood of street noises and damp air. It closed. Cally looked around to see a tall man, his back to her, wiping rain off his face with both hands. Then he gave himself a vigorous shake, spraying drops from his jacket and off a thatch of shaggy dark hair. He looked like a Labrador retriever just emerged from a lake.

So, art had won out over comfort. She watched him, intrigued. Why had he taken so long to make up his mind?

When he turned it was quick, as if to catch whoever was staring at him. Knowing how rude she must look, yet unwilling to be stared down, she studied him openly.

It was a dark, hard face with eyes of a light, indeterminate colour. He looked a few years older than herself, perhaps just short of thirty. The plain navy jacket, white buttoned shirt and grey flannels were neat and conventional.

Too conventional. He radiated such an aura of contained power that the unremarkable clothes might have been a disguise. He was a piece of the storm invading the gallery's civilized stillness. Yet he hadn't moved or spoken, simply returned her stare. A quirk of tight muscles in one cheek signalled that he found her either annoying or funny.

I must look shameless — goggling at the man!

Cally flashed him a smile that blended amusement, apology and

— why not? — appreciation. Then she turned and walked into the next room.

And nearly walked right out again. This was the main part of Sheila's exhibition. The walls were crowded with body parts. Clenched fists, angry eyes, a set mouth showing teeth. A foreboding heaviness hit the pit of her stomach.

The last of the visitors had left. Noel and Sheila sat together on a low wooden bench, watching her and waiting for her reaction. She sat down beside Sheila and touched her hand. "I wish I could say I love this."

Sheila gave her a defiant look from under dark eyebrows. "The reviews have been good."

"Stunningly good," Noel put in.

"I'm working something out. That's what this is about."

Noel reached around Sheila to touch Cally reassuringly on the elbow. He, if anyone, ought to know when his sister was all right.

They were twins, although no twins could have been less alike. She was dark where he was fair, she was thin-skinned and plain-spoken while he was a born diplomat. She was usually too absorbed in her work to fuss with her appearance, which probably bothered him more than anything. The stylishly cut dress she wore for her first public showing had been Noel's selection, not hers.

"Why have you made these female figures look so passive, so...." Cally jumped up and went to get a closer look. "So, well, dead?" She shook her head as she walked along the walls. "The male figures are all so threatening. This one holds a stone like it's a weapon. This one...." She grimaced.

Sheila shrugged. "In that one, the fist is the weapon."

"I hope that's not a statement about relationships between the sexes. Because — oh...."

4

The words died in her mouth. She had stopped in front of the largest painting. Its impact froze her to the spot and sent a shiver through her. This had to be the best work Sheila had ever done. And yet, and yet....

The man in the picture stood with his back to the viewer, fists clenched at his sides, feet set solidly yet dangerously on the very brink of a cliff. Beyond him, a battlement of dark clouds towered up beyond an expanse of lead-coloured water. A sense of pent-in violence ran along the taut lines of the body, focusing in the powerful shoulders and in the head, which was caught in the act of turning to look back. A white patch showing against the clothing proved to be a playing card sticking out of the back pocket of the jeans. An ace of spades.

Cally stood frowning at this portrait until a change in the air told her that another person was in the room. She looked around. It was the man who'd come in out of the rain. Sheila and Noel stood up. Noel's face was wary, Sheila's pinched with — was that anger or fear? Cally gazed back and forth, perplexed.

The man strolled along the walls, ignoring the other three. As Cally watched him she suddenly felt the disorientation that comes from seeing yourself in a room full of mirrors. Except that it was him she was seeing endlessly repeated, not herself.

The pictured eyes, the tight mouth, the straight nose, the scowling black brows — all his. The shoulders, the shape of the head. She glanced down at his large, well-shaped, capable-looking hands, and remembered the hand on the poster at the door. And the man on the cliff, with the ace of spades in his pocket, that was him too.

What the hell?

Cally turned to Sheila, only to see her face tighten up. Cally turned again to find the stranger planted right in front of her and staring over her shoulder at Sheila.

"It's time we had this out." His deep voice was dangerously quiet. "I always knew you had no use for me. But this—" He swung an arm wide around the room. "Sheila, we've got to talk about this."

Sheila pressed back against Noel's arm. Her eyes never left the man's face. Trapped between Sheila and the newcomer, Cally felt as if she'd unexpectedly come face to face with a grizzly in the woods.

"Leave her alone!" Noel's tone was aggressive.

"What's going on?" Cally demanded. Nobody answered.

The man's face hardened. His hand fell. He made a dismissive gesture and turned his back on them. Then strode to the nearest wall and wrenched off the stiff acrylic sheet covering one of the larger ink studies, ignoring Noel's indignant protest. It was a finely detailed drawing of a man — himself — arrogantly standing over the prone body of a woman. He snatched the drawing off the wall.

Lines deepened around his mouth. He grasped the top edge of the paper. Next instant, Cally's hands cupped his two fists. She stared at him over the paper barrier.

"Don't you dare!"

His eyes were brilliant with fury and with something else, deeper, which she couldn't interpret. And they were grey as November rain. The hard muscles of his hands bunched under hers.

"Don't do it — unless you want to pay five hundred dollars for the privilege of tearing it up!"

For the first time since entering the room, he really saw her. The bleak eyes warmed, the thick brows lifted. He lowered the picture. "Five hundred? Isn't that a bit steep?"

"It isn't for sale," Sheila said faintly.

Cally tipped her head back at Sheila. "You heard her. Not for sale. The five hundred's to cover damages. It *was*. Now it's a thou-

6

sand."

He stared, incredulous; then laughed. "Thank God for you, who-ever you are." He was suddenly a different man: attractive, pleasant, at ease.

"Cally Macdonald." She held out a hand. He gripped it a mo-ment, smiling. Then offered her the picture.

"Hold this for me? Thanks." He pulled a chequebook and gel pen from the inside pocket of his jacket, placed a large oxford-shod foot on the bench and used his knee as a writing desk.

"You're right, it's much too good to destroy." He tore off the cheque and handed it to her, retrieved the picture, rolled it up and thrust it inside his jacket. Then walked carelessly to the door, where he turned and looked back.

"So long, Noel. Sheila. See you on the island." Then with a faint smile: "You too, Cally." A stride, and he was gone. The room was all at once quiet and empty.

"Amazing!" Noel laughed. "I've never seen him back down like that before. You must have some special magic, Cally."

"But who was he?"

Sheila sat slumped on the bench. She looked exhausted. Cally glanced at the cheque in her hand and whistled. "Wow, it really is for a thousand dollars!" The signature was black and emphatic, yet neatly formed. "Matthew Forrest?"

When nobody met her eyes, she laid the cheque on the bench be-side Sheila. Then took Noel firmly by the arm and walked him into the next room, where the gallery director was dimming the lights.

"It's over. A great success all round!" She beamed at them and returned to her office. They had the big, cold room to themselves.

"So," said Cally. "That was the invisible brother."

"Yes, that was our beloved Matthew. I suppose you had to come across him sooner or later. Of course he's not really our brother." Seeing her perplexed look he added, "He was adopted."

"I didn't know that. Sheila almost never mentions him. I was starting to think he was imaginary, a sort of monster under the bed."

"In a way, he is. Didn't you notice how different he is? Not one of us. He's always been an outsider, really."

Cally felt an unexpected stab of sympathy for Matthew. "Isn't that rather unfair? How old was he when he was adopted?"

"Just a baby. My parents had given up on having children of their own. If only they'd had the patience to wait a few more years, till Sheila and I came along!" He forced a smile. "I'm sorry, Cally. It really wasn't fair to drop you into this situation. Before you accepted our proposal we should have warned you he'd be with us on the island."

"But what's her problem with him? Those pictures, what's with them?"

"They're only images. Still, if you want to back out, I won't blame you one bit."

Cally walked back to where she could see into the next room. Sheila still sat on the bench, hands clasped on her knees, head bent. Her silky dark hair was escaping from its clasp, as it usually did. She looked like an abandoned twelve-year-old.

The sight of her brought back their first day at TCU, nearly six years ago. Everything was new then, everybody was a stranger, the whole world was chaos. Cally had been unpacking in her residence room and wondering hopefully what her roommate would be like. She'd looked up to see Sheila in the doorway, a thin dark girl lugging an art portfolio half her height. Her eyes were black with what Cally at first thought was fury. Then she looked again and saw misery, and heard the unspoken cry for help that everybody else had missed. She

8

slipped an arm around Sheila's rigid shoulders and guided her into the room. "I have double chocolate brownies from home," she announced, "enough for an army, and I can't possibly eat them all myself. Wanna help?"

Despite being nothing alike the two had stayed close friends ever since, even during the last two years since leaving residence and living apart.

"Fact is," Noel said quietly, "she hasn't yet gotten over Dad's death last year."

Cally looked at him worriedly. "Then maybe I shouldn't come. Maybe she needs to be alone."

"No way — I want you there!" Sheila joined them and linked her arm in Cally's. "Remember your promise, Cal. Didn't you always say you'd be there for me when I need you?"

"So I did." She couldn't help smiling at Sheila's serious face.

"Well, I need you now. Maybe now more than ever. Cally, you're my friend. Please come!"

"Oh, of course I'll come!" They hugged. Noel beamed.

Chapter 2

HE MUST HAVE BEEN waiting across the street, watching as the three of them came out of the gallery and put up their umbrellas. The twins offered a lift. Cally turned it down, meaning to shop for a new swimsuit before going home. He caught up with her at the corner of Dundas and Boyden.

"We need to talk," he said.

She studied his expression, which told her nothing. Then shrugged. "Okay, but not out here in the rain. I know a pub." She tilted her umbrella. "Thataway."

Cally had always liked the honest dinginess of the dark little tavern on Boyden Road, one of the maze of shabby downtown streets around the university. No hanging plants, no artsy odds and ends, no upscale nonsense. A good place to hang out with friends and classmates on a Saturday night. But today for the first time she wished it were better lit. The small, rather grimy windowpanes let in little of the late afternoon light. It was hard to read the man's expression.

"I think you knew about me," she said, as their beers arrived. "About my coming to the island, I mean."

"Ginny told me. Old friend of Sheila's, are you?"

"Uh-huh. And Noel's. That's why I'm curious. How come I know so little about you?"

"Maybe they're trying to protect you."

He left it hanging in the air. Her brows wrinkled. Briskly he went on, "In any case, Cally, Stone Face Island is an isolated place. This is not Muskoka, it's not the fun-among-the-pines resort you're probably thinking of. There's no cellphone coverage, no internet, no wifi. You can only get there by boat, the generator breaks down at the damnedest times—"

"I know. Sheila's told me. I can tough it out without wifi." She was laughing at him, ever so gently.

"It's a place you might find it hard to get away from," he said quietly. "If you ever wanted to leave in a hurry."

"Why would I want to leave in a hurry?"

"You just might."

"Are you trying to get rid of me?" She'd tried to keep things light, but her patience was wearing thin.

He stared at her over the rim of his glass. "Cally. What the hell kind of name is that?"

"It's Scottish. It's short for Catriona."

"Shouldn't the short form be Catty?"

"No, it should not!"

He kept staring, and at that moment the sun split the clouds and sent a wave of gold through the window. It picked out chestnut glints in his dark hair and a hint of blue in his grey eyes. And showed fine lines around his mouth and eyes that looked like they came from fatigue, or pain.

She found herself gazing, and switched her eyes away. "Oh, great!" She peered out at the flying clouds. "We'll have good weather to start, at least."

"What makes you think you're qualified to tutor a kid like Ginevra?"

The change of subject made her blink. "You mean, aside from the teaching qualification I earned last year, and the degree in English language and literature I earned the year before that?"

He made a throwing-away gesture with one hand. "Pieces of paper."

"Then how about my two semesters as a teaching assistant, cattle-driving first-year engineers toward a grasp of basic grammar?"

"Better. Anything else?"

"I have three younger brothers, all much bigger than me. They learned to jump when I said so." She flashed a mean smile.

His lips quirked. "Huh. But how well do you know Ginevra?"

"Not well. I met her a couple of times when your father was alive. And I know a bit about that accident, and her disability. And yes, she's a handful."

"Hm. Well." He opened his hands, as if letting something go. "Maybe, just maybe, you can do it. You've got some starch in you. You'll need it!"

"Um ... Matthew." She gripped the edge of the table with both hands. "Can we get something straight?"

He just looked at her. She went on: "Noel is Ginevra's guardian, not you. Am I right? He was the one who hired me, and not just because I'm an old friend."

"But he isn't the one who knows Ginny best." The lines deepened around his mouth. Before she could think of a reply he changed the subject again. "You and your three brothers. Do you get along?"

"Get along? Oh, sure. We squabble, and they try to push me around, and I whack them into line." She laughed. "At least, we squabbled when we were kids. Now it's just for fun. We learned to stick by each other after our father died, we learned to help our mom. That's why I find you Forrests such a puzzle."

"We don't get along." He almost smiled. "That's partly what this July on the island is all about. All of us learning to get along. As our father willed."

Willed. An odd way to put it. "Well, I don't see why you

12

shouldn't get along. You're not so awful. I saw you outside, you know."

"Outside?"

"Outside the gallery. You spent a lot of time working up your courage to come in. I could see that. I'm guessing you knew what sort of welcome to expect, but you came anyway, because you wanted to see your sister's first show. And somehow I can't square that with what I saw in the pictures. Somebody, somewhere, has got some wires crossed. Either Sheila's made a terrible mistake, or she's suffering from delusions — which I don't believe — or...."

He stared at her grimly.

"Or else she has real reason to fear you." She held his eyes. "What on earth did you do to her?"

"I can't think of a blessed thing."

"But you must have done something."

"She's always been rather fragile. You must know that. She's afraid of a lot of things. Big dogs. Bats. Driving on the 401." He pushed his beer glass back and forth on the table. "Why she chose my image to express her fears, I just don't know."

"This is upsetting you, isn't it?" She watched as he dug first in one coat pocket, then in another. "What are you looking for?"

"What's not there. I quit smoking weeks ago but I still automatically reach for a coffin-nail when...."

"When you're upset," she finished for him. "No wonder you're so tense. Quitting smoking can be very stressful."

"I'm not tense!" He certainly sounded tense. He leaned across the table, his pale eyes flickering in the changing light from the windows. "Look! For all our sakes, I'm telling you not to come to the island."

"Why?"

"It's too complicated to explain. Just take it from me: there'll be trouble, and you'll only make it worse."

"Why?"

For a moment she thought he was going to reach across and....
"Grabbing and shaking me," she said evenly, "won't do you an ounce
of good. Suppose you try explaining yourself instead?"

"Waste of breath! It's too obvious whose side you're on."

"I think," she said serenely, "you could all get along quite nicely
if you'd only try."

"I give up!" He drained his glass and banged it down on the table. His chair screeched back. "See you soon, Miss Pollyanna. I just
hope you don't find your island junket too unpleasant."

Chapter 3

STONE FACE ISLAND lay two miles across Lake St. Jude from the village of Blackwater Bay. Its ragged profile rose from a sandy beach in the east to high, bare cliffs in the west. The forest-roughened slopes were intensely green, the choppy water a dance of diamonds under the sun of early July. The sky above the island was a blue almost too deep for nature.

"It looks magical," Cally said. "It's a picture out of a kids' storybook."

"Yeah, sure, now it looks good." Jack Beamish's leathery face was set in pessimistic grooves. "But you wait till it rains, eh? Hope you got some warm clothes in them bags."

He throttled up the outboard and the small white boat leaped forward, banging down hard on the swells and ripping out sheets of spray. The wind flung cold water in Cally's face and whipped wet strands of hair into her eyes. She shook them away and laughed, exhilarated. Jack hunched his shoulders distastefully. She guessed he would have liked to see her clutching the gunwale in fright.

He cut speed as the boat curved in toward the island and cruised north, past the western end. Here the steep slopes were less thickly wooded. The rocky tip was bare. There was no sign of a house.

"There!" Jack slowed the boat still more and stabbed his forefinger up at the cliff. "That's how the island got her name. There's the stone face. See it?"

The cliff was hundreds of feet high, Cally estimated: an expanse of granite worn smooth by weather, seamed with fissures and craggy with outcrops. She searched for a face as the boat passed. Each moment a new perspective slid into view and showed a different pattern of highlights and shadows. She shook her head. "No, I don't."

And then, there it was. A heavy brow ridge over deep eye pits, long straight nose, flat cheekbones. A wide glum mouth, the upper lip jutting over the lower, a hollow between them as if the stony lips had parted for breath. Sheared-off chin and undercut throat, then fifty feet straight down to the boulder-strewn beach.

For three uneasy seconds she saw the whole tip of the island as a giant head rising out of the water to peer at her. Imagination easily added the giant's body stretched below the surface.

She blinked, and the boat moved on, and the cliff was just a tall slab of fissured granite.

"Wait, what's that thing on top?" She shaded her eyes and squinted against the sun. A flattened shape squatted a few yards back from the brink of the cliff. At first sight it looked like a natural stone formation. Then she made out a chimney and a slanting roof, and beneath deep eaves the black slits of windows, like the vertical pupils in a cat's eyes.

It gave Cally a start. "That's not where I'll be staying, is it? I thought the house was white. And bigger."

"Cottage," Jack growled. "House is the other end." He swung the boat out and back in a loop and ran it eastward, parallel with the southern shore.

"Cottage! But who would live there? It must be a hundred years old!"

"Nah. The house is a hundred. Cottage is three hundred."

Cally did a double take over her shoulder. "Three hundred! But I thought this region wasn't even settled till 1850 or thereabouts."

"It wasn't. Not by what you'd call real settlers. But there was

16

people here all the same."

"You mean, besides First Nations people?"

"Yeah, yeah." He looked annoyed. "My great-great-granddad owned that little house, so I should know."

He kept up an offended silence as they followed the shore. At last, toward the eastern end of the island, Cally spotted a break in the woods high on a hillside, and a promising glimmer of white.

Matthew was waiting for them on the pier. He had exchanged his urban disguise for wear-softened jeans and a torn grey sweatshirt that was years past hope of repair. His hair hung shaggily over his forehead and he looked as if he hadn't shaved since she'd last seen him, two days before.

"Any mail?" he said to Jack, eliminating her first, pleasurable idea that he'd come down to greet her.

"Oh, yeah." Jack fumbled in a steel box at his feet. He picked out two or three envelopes, set them carefully on the pier above his head, then awkwardly pulled out a small cardboard box. It seemed to be heavy for its size.

"Here's your package." He rose, crouching, and held it out just beyond Matthew's reach. Matt knelt on the planks and put out a hand, but suddenly Jack staggered. He thrust his arms wide to regain his balance, and the package flew into the air. It hit the water with a splash and was instantly gone.

Jack sat down again. "Oh, gee, what a shame! I'm real sorry."

Cally wondered how anyone could be so clumsy. When she looked up at Matthew, his eyes were blazing silver. He started to speak, bit off the words, and took a deep breath. Jack bent over the suitcases, not quite hiding a smirk.

"Can't we get it back?" Cally asked. "With a scoop net or something?"

"No. I'll have to dive for it."

Matthew pulled his sweatshirt over his head and dropped it on the boards, uncovering a tanned, muscular chest that widened into powerful shoulders. Cally told herself not to stare, then stared. He bent to pull off tattered sneakers. Next went the socks. Cally's eyes widened as his hands went to the zipper of his pants and he began to peel them off.

He caught her eye. "So? You try swimming in jeans and see how far you get." Then the jeans were on the pier in a heap, *but thank God not the briefs,* Cally thought, and he was a six-foot javelin of bronze and white cotton, slicing the air. The water parted for him and closed over him neatly. And kept him so long that she began to peer anxiously over the gunwale. It seemed a frighteningly long time before his head broke the surface, spraying water in all directions. He gulped air, upended and disappeared again.

By now Jack had manhandled the suitcases out of the boat, and seemed in a hurry to be on his way. After yanking Cally up the short ladder onto the pier, he picked up one of the cases — the smaller one — and loped away toward the sandy beach. She trudged after him with the larger one. Every few steps she took a look back, only relaxing when she saw Matt climb back onto the pier with something heavy in one hand.

They followed a smooth rock-dust path that looped up through speckled sunshine under the trees. At the top, a velvety emerald lawn stretched toward a big, contented-looking Victorian house shining white in its frame of roses and cedars.

Sheila met her at the front door, dressed in shorts over a bathing suit. "Thanks, Jack, I'll take it from here." He dropped the case with a thud in the hall and stumped off toward the rear of the house: the kitchen, Cally guessed, by the sounds and smells. She sniffed appreciatively.

Sheila smiled. "Yes, we're lucky to have Mrs. Gardner, she's a wonderful cook. We're not so lucky with Jack, but...." She shrugged and let it go. "Come on up to your room. You'll love it."

It was a lovable room, painted a pale leaf-green and comfortably crowded with old-fashioned white-enameled furniture. Sunshine flooded in through the tall double window, which opened like a pair of doors onto a small iron-railed balcony.

Cally had to step out at once and savour the view. Below lay the flagstone terrace that surrounded the house, then the crisply shaped flower beds and the lush perfection of the lawn. Beyond the lawn to the west, the forest started up again. Its wild tangle rose for half a mile to the island's crest. The cottage was just visible as a boxy shape beyond the farthest trees.

And all around lay the lake, like a swatch of blue silk wrapping it all together. Cally filled her lungs with the clean, rose-scented air. A faint tinkle of music came to her ears: someone playing a piano in one of the rooms below. It was the perfect, completing touch.

"It's too idyllic," she said as she stepped back inside. "There has to be a worm in the bud."

"There will be, don't worry." Sheila sat on the bed and watched as Cally unpacked and put away her belongings.

"If you mean Matthew, you've got me puzzled. I don't see what the problem is. She turned from the dresser and sat down beside Sheila on the bed. "To be honest, I think there's an awful lot you aren't telling me."

"Well ... maybe." Sheila rubbed at an ink stain on her thumb.

"And it seems to me, if you want my moral support, it's a bit unfair to keep me in the dark." Cally didn't feel hopeful, though. Despite their long-standing friendship, there had always been dark corners in Sheila's life, places she stored her fears and sorrows, where even a best friend was hardly ever admitted.

Sheila slid off the bed and went to the window. "I'll have to apologize ahead of time, Cal. I won't be at my best, here on the island. Truth is, I hate the place."

"Hate this beautiful place?" Cally glanced at the glowing vista framed in the tall rectangle of the windows.

"I've hated it for years. I only ever came because Dad was here every summer. But now with Dad gone, I have no reason to come back. I'm only here for Noel and Gin."

"But how could you hate it?"

"Bad memories, I guess." Sheila leaned against the window frame and gazed westward. "Mother spent her last months here. Then there was what happened to Francesca. Then Ginevra."

Francesca: a seldom mentioned name. Cally had to grope through her recollections for it. Francesca Gioberti, George Forrest's second wife. Young, convent-educated, a redhead from Milan. Married three years after George's first wife's death from cancer, and Ginevra was born three years after that. Some people, Noel for one, were surprised the marriage lasted as long as it did.

"You never liked her, did you?" Cally probed gently, not sure how far she could go.

"How could we?" Sheila shot her an angry glance. "It wasn't just his marrying again. If only he'd picked somebody suitable! But no, it had to be a girl of nineteen. And he was nearly fifty, for Pete's sake! They had absolutely nothing in common. I still don't understand what got into him!"

Cally opened her mouth to suggest possible explanations. For example, that Francesca had been drop-dead gorgeous, by all accounts. And who knew, maybe they'd loved each other. But Sheila didn't want to hear it and besides, that tragedy was years past. There was no cure for it now.

"What exactly happened to her?"

Sheila was silent. She disliked talking about Francesca, and Cally had never pressed her. She only had an impression that there had been an accident, and the shock of it had brought on their father's first heart attack. He had never fully recovered, physically or emotionally.

Another name surfaced in Cally's recollections. "Vanessa. Remember her? Did Noel ever find out where she went?"

Vanessa Hurst had been Noel's girlfriend when he was still an undergrad. Cally hadn't liked her much, too high-toned and high-powered, but Noel had made up his mind she was the one. Then only months later she'd broken it off and gone away. "Am I wrong, or was this the last place she was seen? The island. She was here, right?"

Sheila turned abruptly from the window. "Any wonder I hate the place? Most of all I hate that old stone cottage. I'm almost ready to believe Jack when he claims it's cursed."

"Cursed!" Cally was diverted. "Is there a story?"

"There are plenty of stories. I wouldn't put stock in any of them. But I'd stay away from there, if I were you."

"No kidding!"

"No, Cally, I'm not kidding. The cliff's dangerous. And the cottage may not be cursed, but it really isn't safe, either. We get vandals, kids from Blackwater Bay, fooling around there with lights, knocking stones out of the chimney, stealing small tools. Last year a bit of the chimney fell down the roof and just missed Noel's head. Of course, Jack says it wasn't vandals, it was his great-great granddad defending his property against marauders."

Cally got up from the bed and carried a stack of underwear and

T-shirts to the chest of drawers. "Well, I'm disappointed. A ghost would've made this island perfect. By the way, who plays the piano?"

"That would be either Aubrey or Gin. She has piano lessons every afternoon."

Cally froze with her hands in the drawer. "Aubrey? Not Aubrey Moscoe?"

"Yes, your Aubrey." A rare smile lit up Sheila's face. "I wanted it to be a surprise."

Cally groaned softly, and started to laugh. Sheila joined in, a little anxiously.

"You knew he was coaching Gin on piano when she wasn't away at that school of hers," she said. "Well, Noel got in touch with him about a month ago and asked him to come to the island for the summer and carry on with the lessons. Noel had forgotten about you and Aubrey, but I hadn't, and I thought it would be fun to ... uh...." She crossed the room and touched Cally's arm. "Cal? You are thrilled, aren't you?"

Cally could only laugh helplessly and shake her head.

"Cal? What's wrong?"

"You knew we were engaged. I guess you didn't know we got disengaged."

"Oh, no! When?"

"New Year's." She slammed the drawer and turned around. "Yeah, I should've told you, but I didn't. Didn't want to admit what a fool I'd been. And I suppose he never told you either."

"Not a peep." Sheila made fists. "And I mentioned the engagement and he didn't correct me. The louse! I'll kill him!"

"Let it go, Sheila. Let him live."

Sheila dropped her hands. "Do you hate me?"

22

"Not a bit!" Cally grabbed her hands and swung them. "It's not the disaster you think. I dumped him, not the other way around. Now that there's a distance between us, I could even like him again. Mildly!"

"Well, that's a relief. Because I like him too — mildly!"

Chapter 4

KNOWING NOEL and his fastidious, oddly old-fashioned notions about proper attire for this and that occasion, Cally took pains to dress nicely for dinner. She put on a long green linen skirt and cream silk blouse with gold belt and sandals, and brushed her cap of straight brown hair to a shine. She felt a little let down to find Matthew was not there. He was up at the cottage as usual, Noel said.

Unexpectedly, she found herself only the second best-dressed woman at the table. Sheila, who hardly ever paid attention to her appearance, had made an effort tonight. She'd pinned her dark hair up in an elegant twist and put on a slim white sheath that made her look like an arum lily.

Ginevra, at Sheila's left, wore a blue cotton sundress that should have been in the laundry, and her nails could have used a scrub. And although she held herself well and her legs looked thin but perfectly normal, it was impossible not to notice the motorized wheelchair in a corner.

And yet she outshone every other female in the room. At eleven her body was still a child's, but her face gave promise of the stunner she would be in a very few years: the face a perfect oval, the features fine, the complexion translucent. Wide-set brown eyes, framed in long dark lashes, gazed boldly out at the world. Her mouth, rosy and full, was already a woman's. Masses of glowing red hair waved and curled around her face and shoulders. Cally felt a sudden, protective urge to tame that luxuriant mane, to confine it safely in a pair of neat braids.

Feeling Cally's gaze, Ginevra smiled sweetly across the table. "I suppose you're wondering about my mother. She was just a girl when Daddy married her, and she was only twenty-seven when she died. It was so tragic. She—"

Noel reached over and tapped her on the wrist. "Gin, not now, please."

She sent him a tremulous glance, then again turned a dreamy look on Cally. "But it *was* tragic. She fell from—"

"What a self-dramatizing little brat you are!" Aubrey laughed. "Look at you! Your hair is in your soup."

Her creamy face darkened. She searched for a wounding reply, but next moment he resumed his flirtation with Sheila.

When Cally had come face to face with him in the front hall before dinner he had called out joyfully, kissed her on the cheek, and showed nothing but delight at the prospect of sharing a house with her. At first she was furious. Their time together, his casual infidelities, and their stormy break-up might never have been. Then she pulled herself together, kissed him back lightly, pushed him away and laughed at him, and this, she thought, pleased him very well.

As soon as they sat down to dinner he caught Sheila's eye and began a light-hearted verbal sparring. And Sheila, Cally was surprised to see, seemed to enjoy it. At least, she didn't retreat into steely silence as she so often did. She laughed and her pale cheeks bloomed with colour. If that was Aubrey's doing, good for him!

Perhaps I'd better warn her, though. Aubrey was very attractive, mostly for his amusing silliness, smiling eyes and expressively mobile face — which was otherwise rather homely, thin and beaky-nosed — in its frame of wild brown curls. Attractive, and absolutely unreliable. And Sheila was so vulnerable.

Cally caught his eye and sent him a warning frown. *Watch your step!* He winked at her.

"AND THIS IS the showpiece of the house." Dinner was over. Noel led the way into the living room — or, as he always called it, the parlour. "Cally, you've just time-travelled to Pittsburgh, 1890."

He waved a hand grandly at the gold brocade walls, the bulging sofas, the dazzling crystal chandelier. "The first owner was a steel baron. I believe this was the height of chic in those days."

Sheila dropped onto a sofa. "It takes my breath away every time I come in here. For sheer brazen ugliness!" She picked up a folio-sized book of wildlife drawings and propped it open on her knees.

"I still say we need a TV," said Ginevra, whirling her wheelchair to a stop in the centre of the room.

Noel shook his head. "Dad always dug his heels in about that, and so will I," he said to Cally. "A television wouldn't suit this house. However, there is a stereo CD player, which Aubrey tells me is almost an antique. It's built into that cabinet near the fireplace, and so it doesn't spoil the look of the place."

"Speaking of music!" Aubrey held out his hands to Ginevra. "It's time Noel found out how much you've improved lately. C'mon and show your stuff."

"Okay, why not?" Ginevra eased her wheelchair in beside the piano bench, folded back an arm rest and used her hands to slide herself from the wheelchair to the bench. She settled herself, threw a look over her shoulder as if to say, "Is everybody paying attention?" and began to play.

Cally didn't know enough about music to identify the piece, but it sounded old and romantic. Ginevra made the most of its cascades and trills. She played marvellously. Too marvellously. Even Cally soon grasped that Ginevra was parodying the piece in order to show off her skill. After a few minutes Aubrey reached across and smartly slapped her hands. "I said play, not muck about!"

Red-faced, she glared at the keyboard. "Just play," Aubrey said quietly. "Do it right. You don't have to prove anything." He pulled out fresh music and set it up on the rack. She stayed mulishly silent for half a minute. Then her face cleared, she nodded and again her hands descended on the keys.

This time Cally knew the piece. It was *Brouillards*, a prelude by Debussy. The performance that followed was as honest as the first had been false. The pensive music was one with the quiet concentration on Ginevra's face.

"Now that," said Aubrey, when it was over, "Was something like your best."

"Bravo!" Noel called, and Cally and Sheila applauded. Aubrey helped Ginevra slide back into her wheelchair, from which she bowed and blew kisses to her adoring fans.

"Now let's have a fire!" she demanded. "I'm freezing!"

"Can't have that, can we?" Noel added to Cally, "Nights can sometimes be chilly here, even in July." He left the room. They heard voices in the hall and then he reappeared in the doorway. "I've sent Jack for wood."

Sheila said: "By the way, he was drunk again this afternoon. We shouldn't let him take the boat out when he's like that."

Noel made a regretful clucking sound.

"He could hurt himself or somebody else," she persisted. "I don't know why we keep him on. I'll bet he pilfers your Scotch."

"I know he does."

"Then why—"

"He's a first-rate gardener, that's why. And more importantly, Father hired him — what is it now? Thirty-odd years ago? He's been helping to take care of things on the island longer than any of us has been alive. I feel we have a family obligation."

Cally asked curiously, "Did Jack's great-great-grandfather really own that cottage?"

"Uh-oh." Noel chuckled. "Has he been at you already? No, Cally, some ancestor of his did live there for a time, but he never legally owned it."

Jack chose this moment to appear in the doorway where he stood glaring around. He carried an armload of split logs. "It *was* his house," he growled.

"We've been through this before, Jack." Noel was indulgent, but he sounded weary.

"It *was* his. Didn't belong to nobody else. That's called squatter's rights. Then along comes the gov'ment, selling off people's land—"

"Come on, Jack, let's get that fire built." Noel bent to slide back the brass mesh curtains. To Cally he added, "He knows perfectly well that the old man's land — which wasn't actually his — wasn't touched. Old Beamish was allowed to keep the top end of the island, but the lower end was sold to a new settler. At which Old Beamish tried to drive him off with a shotgun."

"That's right." Jack grinned. "My great-granddad shot the new guy dead. So they hung'm."

"And they say his spirit *walks*." Ginny said in an eerie voice. "Right, Jack?"

"Well, wouldn't you, if they stole your house and then hung you?"

Cally studied Jack's leathery face as he set to work building up the fire. Did he really believe this hooey? "D'you mean people have actually seen a ghost?"

"Yeah, sure. I seen him once myself, through a window. He was sitting down, having a drink."

Aubrey began to laugh. Jack flared up. "Oh, call me a liar! Ask anybody. Lots of people seen him. He sits by an oil lantern," he said to Cally. "People seen the light."

"What they've seen," Noel broke in impatiently, "was the same kind of 'ghost' who loosened the stone last year that nearly brained me."

Jack rose creakily to his feet, gave Noel a baleful look, and tramped out of the room. Cally stretched her feet luxuriously toward the crackling flames.

"Well, don't you want to hear the rest of the story?" Noel settled into an armchair facing her. "Old Man Beamish's widow sold her portion to the new settler's heirs, making it one island again, then she and her children moved to Blackwater Bay. Jack has no legal claim at all. The new people sold out to the Pittsburgh steel man who built this house in 1890, and my grandfather bought the island in 1946."

"For my great-grandmother," Ginevra said, gazing dreamily into the fire. "It was a wedding present for his lovely young bride."

"That's right, Gin." Noel smiled at her. "And we've been here ever since, every summer."

Cally sniffed. "What I'd really like to know is whether Jack believes all that about the ghost, or whether he was just pulling very hard on my leg."

"Oh, he believes it. Around these parts they all do."

"Is the cottage actually three centuries old? Or is that more embroidery?"

"That," Noel said, "may actually be close to the truth. It was here long before the British conquest, we know that. There's a bit about the island in the *Jesuit Relations*. Sheila, you recall it."

Sheila's book slammed shut. "You're not going to drag out that horrible story again, are you?"

"It's only history, Sheila."

"It's not. It's here and now, and we all know it. Oh, go ahead, tell it. Cally should be warned." Sheila curled up in a corner of the sofa and wrapped her arms around her bent knees. Quietly, Cally left her place by the fire and sat down on the sofa beside Sheila. She could feel her trembling. "Why don't we forget about the story for now?"

"No, you ought to know. It's a dangerous place. I can feel it and so can Noel, if he'd only admit it."

"Whatever happened is in the past," Cally said matter-of-factly. "That doesn't mean it has to happen again."

"Oho, you think so!" Ginevra swirled her wheelchair back and forth. "What about the curse, then? There really is one, you know."

"I don't believe in curses," Cally said lightly. "Except maybe in stories."

"Well, this is a true story, and if nobody else will tell it, I will. It started with the Indian Wars — right, Noel? — when there was a Huron village up on that end of the island. And a bunch of Iroquois came and massacred them, every single one. The ground," she said with relish, "was *soaked* with their innocent blood! And the Iroquois *ate* them, and put their heads up on poles! And it's been *cursed* ever since that day!"

"But if they were all killed," Cally asked reasonably, "how did the story come out?"

"Oh, one did get away. In a canoe. And then he told the priests and they wrote the story down. So it's true."

"Oh, Ginny! One of these days...." Sheila scrubbed at her face, forced a smile and sat up. "I'm overtired. Guess I'll go to bed."

As she spoke, an ornate long-case clock in one corner bonged ten times.

Cally stood up. "I'll go up with you."

"Thanks, Cal, but I'm fine, really. Stay by the fire." She waved and was gone.

"But not you, Miss Ginevra." Noel pointed a long forefinger.

Ginevra shivered theatrically. "But I'm cold! Why can't I stay by the fire?"

"In bed you'll be warm. Go on, now!"

"Sounds good to me," Cally said. "I'm all in." She offered a general goodnight, then followed a grumbling Ginevra out of the room and along the hall to a small elevator near the kitchen. This, Gin said, was her own private lift. "My father had it put in after my accident. You can use it too, if you ask nicely."

She buzzed inside, her hands brisk and efficient on the controls. The steel doors closed on her, leaving Cally alone in the hall. She turned toward the stairs and had just reached their foot when Aubrey came out of the parlour and closed the door behind him. He looked particularly alive and attractive just then.

"You've been pretty cold, Cally, haven't you?"

"What else would you expect?"

"You mean you're still mad? After all these months?"

"No, I'm mad because you pulled a fast one on Sheila, making her think we were still engaged. Why?"

"Use your noodle! I need this job and I figured she'd get me canned if she found out we'd split."

"Well, I told her. She wanted to kill you, but I saved your hide. So I expect you to behave like a—"

"You darling!" He pulled her close and cut off her protest with a long, thorough kiss on the mouth.

After a moment of stunned outrage she gathered her wits and pushed him off. Raising her head to tell him just what she thought of him, she found herself gazing over his shoulder straight into the eyes of Matthew Forrest. Her cheeks flared.

Aubrey stood aside, looking mischievously from one to the other. "Oh my! It's been so long," he murmured. "Good night, dearest. Sleep well!" He laughed and ran lightly up the stairs.

"That one needs his ears pinned back." The grey eyes were still intent on her face, focused as a searchlight.

"Oh, he doesn't mean a thing by it." She silently cursed her tendency to flush under stress, an albatross she'd hoped to shed in her teens, but never had.

"How well do you know him?"

"Too well."

"What does that mean?"

"Does it matter?" she snapped.

"Guess not." His stare switched off. "Missed my supper," he muttered, and brushed past her to the kitchen.

Chapter 5

CALLY WAS OVER-STIMULATED, confused and tired. Too tired to sleep. She closed her paperback mystery and lay wide-eyed in the darkness for a restless hour. Finally she pushed aside the coverlet and went to the double window, catching up her dressing gown on the way. She sashed its velour folds about her waist and slipped her feet into slippers against the chill of the floor.

The curtains hung open. The tall window framed a piece of moonless black sky, very different from the light-hazed city nights she was used to. She opened the window and stepped out, and the blackness broke up into gradations of dark. The western end of the island shaped a snout-like silhouette that bit upward into the net of brilliant stars.

The stars! She'd never seen anything more wonderful. The night's dark beauty soaked into her mind. Scents teased her nose: the honey sweetness of alyssum, the cool stony smell of the lake. She drew in a deep breath and let it out.

"Can't sleep, Cally?"

She jumped. Matthew's voice came directly from her right. For a moment she thought he must be standing on the balcony beside her, then realized he was on his own balcony, about six feet to the right of hers. He was visible only as a shadow among shadows, leaning on the house wall next to his unlit window. A fiery dot pulsed brightly, then darkened, and she smelled tobacco smoke.

"I thought you quit that filthy habit."

"I did. I started again."

"Don't you know—"

"How bad it is for me? Sure." There was a laugh in his voice.

"Bad for everybody around you, too. Ever hear of second-hand smoke?"

"You can go back inside if it bothers you."

"I don't want to go back inside. By the way, what was in that package?"

"The one Jack tried to drown?" The fiery dot described a plunge in the darkness. "Square nails."

"Square what?"

"I'm restoring the cottage. Want to do it right. Back when it was built, they used iron nails that were square in cross-section."

"You're restoring it all by yourself? But it's such an old building! Isn't that a job for an expert?"

"I am an expert," he said dryly. "It's the way I make my living. I'm an architect."

"I didn't know that." She frowned. "There's so much I don't know about you, and...." *And I'd very much like to know.* Her cheeks flared again. She was glad it was dark. "This cottage must be fascinating," she finished quickly.

"Come up and see me some time." His voice sounded amused. You'd think he could hear a blush. "I'll show you around."

"I'd like that. When—" She broke off as a distant gleam of light caught her eye. In that ocean of darkness, the single flash was startling. "Did you see that?" Again a golden gleam showed through the farthest trees, one flash and gone. "There it is again! Could it be a boat on the lake?"

"No. Too high. It's on the island."

"Then it must be somebody working in the cottage."

"*Nobody* works in the cottage except me." He ducked back into

34

his room. Cally followed his example, dashed to her door and flung it open in time to see him, denim jacket half on and half off, flying down the stairs.

It was irresistible. She ran back into her room to kick off her slippers and jam on a pair of moccasins. No time to dress. She hitched up the skirts of her robe and gave chase.

She caught up with him near the crest of the island after a stumbling, scrambling climb through the tangled blackness under the trees. When she came upon him, standing still at the edge of a clearing, he turned on her.

"Who — oh, you. What are you doing here?"

"I'm coming with you. You might need help."

He made a sound that was half angry, half amused, and turned back to study the height ahead. The wind stirred a branch. Again came the golden flicker, again it was hidden.

Cally nudged his elbow. "Shouldn't we get going? Won't they escape?"

"Not your problem. Go on back!"

"No. I'll stay in the rear if you insist. But I'm coming with you. And you might try communicating in something other than a snarl."

He let out a breath of laughter. "Okay, I deserved that. I won't waste my time arguing. Just get this into your head. I tried to catch this creep last night and I lost him. So will you — please — be quiet!"

"Of course," Cally said primly.

He set off cat-footed through the trees, pushing aside the branches with care, not letting them snap back. Excitement fluttered in Cally's throat. As they came nearer, the light shone before them like a beacon: warm, inviting, not at all ghostly.

The trees thinned out. Matt halted at the edge of a sweep of turf.

Beyond and above rose the squat shape of the cottage, dead black against the stars. One narrow window glowed. Then it went dark.

He was off the mark like a sprinter. Cally raced after him. They rounded the corner of the building and jostled to a halt a few paces from the door, which stood open. He laid a warning hand on her arm. Then he took a small flashlight from his pocket, switched it on and stooped under the low lintel. She slipped in after him.

The beam ran across walls, into corners, into the deep cave of the fireplace. Nothing moved, nothing made a sound. Muttering, he poked the flashlight at Cally and picked up something from near the door. A click: and a dazzling beam lit up the opposite wall. It was a big battery-powered floodlight.

"Now, let's have a better look."

Because of the thickness of the stone walls, the cottage was much smaller inside than out. It was also lower than Cally had expected, built for a generation of shorter people. There was no ceiling below the roof, but the roughly planed joists were so low that Matt had to walk about with his head bent. He seemed used to it.

The room they stood in took up the entire floor space, and was perhaps twenty feet wide and half as deep. Cardboard boxes and lumber stood in neat stacks against the plank-sheathed walls, along with tools and equipment in orderly rows, all protected by plastic sheeting.

Matt swung the light around the room, his urgency evaporated. No vandal could be hiding here. There was no place to hide. And only one way out: the door. The unglazed windows, with their heavy shutters set back against the inner walls, were barely six inches wide.

Which left unanswered the question of how the vandal had escaped unseen.

"The ghost has vanished!" Cally whispered dramatically, trying not to feel let down.

Matt made a derisive sound. Then his beam caught the glitter of glass below one of the windows. "There!" A hurricane lamp. He picked it up and shook it. Fuel sloshed inside. Cally touched the chimney, then snatched her hand away.

"It's still hot!"

"And here." He nudged something with his shoe. An empty whisky bottle rolled into the light.

"The ghost," Cally murmured, "sits and drinks by the light of a lantern."

"The hell he does. This is Glenlivet, right out of the cabinet in the parlour."

"Okay, so it was Jack. There goes my ghost story. But how did he get away so fast?"

"When I catch him, believe me, he'll tell."

Cally felt flat. The hoax hadn't even been a clever one. She tightened the sash of her dressing gown, aware of the night's chill now that her adrenaline boost was gone. Was it just nerves, or was the air inside the cottage actually colder than outside?

"What a place!" She shivered.

"What's wrong with it? I like it. It's a marvel of classic building methods. It'll stand forever, if those yahoos from the village don't knock it down stone by stone."

"But it's not a home at all, it's a, a protective shell. Look at those shutters on the inside, instead of the outside. They're meant to keep out people, not weather. Whoever built this—"

"Must have been mad? Why? Maybe he was just cautious. Life was rough in those days."

"How did you know I was going to say 'mad'?"

"I figured you'd have it from Sheila by now. She declares she can

37

feel madness oozing from the very stones." He flashed her a grin over the floodlight beam. In the upward-spreading glow, the effect was sinister. "That's it. Tour's over."

He switched off the floodlight and set it down. Then, taking the small flashlight from her hand, he strode out the door. She paused to take one more look around, and jumped as the door slammed shut.

Darkness fell like a black velvet bag over her head: soft, blinding and suffocating. She stood paralyzed. Her imagination remembered the mysterious 'ghost' and shaped a vision of something uncurling in a corner, rising up and sliding silently toward her.

She took three steps in what she hoped was the direction of the door. Her groping hands met wood and found a metal handle. It wouldn't open. She shook it, she pushed hard. He'd locked her in!

Cold air breathed on the back of her neck. A shriek welled up in her throat.

"Stop pushing." Matt's deep voice outside cut across her panic. "Pull. The door opens inward."

Cally yanked it open and fell out.

After the blackness inside the cottage, the starlit night shone like polished crystal. She faced into the breeze, inhaling its cool freshness. She was quivering with reaction to fright: a sweeping anger at Matthew and at herself.

She spun to face him. "You could have waited for me! I might have tripped and sprained something!"

"No danger of that. I keep a tidy shop." He latched the door, which had no lock. "Scared of the dark, Cally? Up until now you gave me the impression there wasn't a thing on this earth you were afraid of." She could just make out his expression. The challenge in it was as clear as a shout. "Was that all just brag and boast, Miss Pollyanna?"

"Are you trying to make enemies?" she asked quietly.

He looked at her a moment, started to answer, then shrugged and walked away. Left alone, Cally was suddenly very much aware of the nearness of the cottage. Its squat shape and the dark mouth of its deep doorway made her think of a tomb.

A restless breeze hummed and whistled through the slit windows. It's like a giant harmonica, she thought. A strange effect but quite natural. Of course.

Then the wind rose and the hum changed to a broken hissing, like malicious laughter. Cally walked and carefully did not run across the meadow.

Matthew was waiting for her at the edge of the woods. She hadn't expected that and was surprised and pleased. *Not such a bear after all.* But when he saw her coming he turned and set off for the house, swinging the flashlight beam on the path ahead of him. She followed the flickering light at a distance of two or three yards. They said nothing to each other.

Reaching the house, he mounted the steps to the terrace. Cally saw him stumble over what looked like a bundle of discarded clothes just short of the front door. He was muttering in disgust as she arrived.

"Look what I found," he growled.

Cally bent to look. The heap of clothes stirred and sent up a reek of whisky. She grimaced and stepped back.

"I'm fed up!" Matt knelt down and shook the bundle. "I could cheerfully wring his neck! I'm sick to death of his tricks and his lies and his sneaking around in the dark! Come on, Jack, get up!"

Cally shot out a hand. "Don't hurt him!"

Matt glared up at her. "I'm not going to hurt him. I'm going to haul his stinking carcass off to bed!"

He stood up, hoisting Jack with him. Then with a grunt he slung the limp body over his shoulder. Cally went ahead to open doors and closed them again behind. They climbed two flights of stairs to the third floor, where Matt carried his burden into a stuffy and cluttered room and dumped it onto the unmade bed.

Then, confounding all her ideas, he arranged Jack in a more or less comfortable position and pulled a blanket over him.

Back on the second floor he paused, hand on the knob of his door, when she caught his sleeve.

"I'm sorry. I shouldn't have thought—"

"Why, did I surprise you by not beating up a helpless drunk? You must have quite an opinion of my character. Next time I'll try to sink to your expectations."

Cally was left staring at his closed door. She wanted to kick herself.

Chapter 6

CALLY MEANT to get an early start on Saturday, but it was nearly noon when she came downstairs. Mrs. Gardner was setting lunch on the table in the breakfast room, which was used for all meals except dinner.

She could hear Ginevra at the piano in the parlour, and Aubrey scolding her for some peccadillo. Noel had been up for five hours. He'd spent the morning in Port Devon, the nearest town of any size, where there was cellphone coverage and wifi, conducting business with his manager in Toronto. He returned in time for lunch. Gin and Aubrey joined them and they went into conference about Ginevra's curriculum over egg, ham and asparagus casserole.

It helped to know that Gin had repudiated her schooling only last Christmas, and that she hadn't rejected all of it. She still did math because she was good at it, and science because she happened to like the science teacher at her school. The rest, she said, was totally useless. "Especially language studies and social studies." Cally's job this summer was to bring Gin up to speed on language studies and social studies.

"Suppose we start with a review of what you learned last fall," Cally said cheerfully, hoping her sunny outlook would rub off on Ginevra. "Then we'll catch up to what you missed. We can explore history and geography through reading and essays."

"Deftly killing four birds with two stones," Noel said. "Very good! Gin, does that suit you?"

Gin made a face. "Sounds sickening."

41

He shook his head at her. "Do you really want to grow up ignorant? Don't you care at all about getting an education?"

"Not really. I already know what I want to do. I'm going to be an international concert pianist. You don't need English and history and all that junk to be a musician."

Cally closed the curriculum file and set it aside. "You do know that you have to go to school until you're sixteen, yes?"

"Yah. Doesn't mean I have to learn anything."

"But you want to go to the Conservatory, right?"

"The Glenn Gould School, actually. So what?" Gin slathered butter on a slice of raisin toast.

"So I'm not sure what the requirements are, but I suspect.... Aubrey?"

"They won't let you in the door without a high school diploma," he said promptly. "Which means you have to finish grades 7 and 8 first."

"Oh." Gin stared glumly at her plate. "I suppose I'll have to do this stuff, then. But don't expect me to act like I enjoy it!" She backed her wheelchair away from the table and buzzed out of the room. There was tragedy in the set of her mouth.

Noel groaned softly, then laughed. "She'll try to make you feel sorry for her, Cally, so you'll go easy on her. Don't let her get away with it!"

"No chance of that! But why was she at the piano today? Are we supposed to have lessons on weekends?"

Aubrey poured himself more coffee. "Nope. My problem's the opposite of yours. She insists we practice at least three hours a day. If Noel didn't stand up for me I'd have no free time at all!"

Just then Sheila came in from sketching, sun-flushed and windblown, her hands still smudged with charcoal. Aubrey poured a cup

42

of coffee and set it in front of her, earning a smile. Noel pushed forward the plate of bread and cheese. "So what's our plan for the afternoon?" he asked.

"Well, if you can stay away from business for an hour or so, I think we should take Cally on a tour of the island." Carelessly Sheila added: "Oh, and Aubrey too, if he likes."

"And me!" said Ginevra, buzzing back into the room so promptly that Cally guessed she had been lurking outside the door, listening. At least she wasn't a sulker.

THEY BEGAN at the eastern end, with its beach of fine sand, its pier and the green and white boathouse that sheltered a canoe and two powerboats: a big red inboard cruiser and the small white aluminum outboard that had ferried Cally from Blackwater Bay.

From the beach they climbed the looping path, which was graded for Ginevra's wheelchair, and crossed the lawn, where Jack was trudging up and down with a push mower. On the side opposite the house, a path led westward into the woods. Cally saw now there had been no call for her to risk her neck scrambling among rocks and undergrowth last night, getting scratched and bitten. Years ago George Forrest had laid down easily navigated paths of hard-packed rock dust from one end of the island to the other.

Except for the paths and the buildings, the island remained much as it had always been. The forest was a wild tangle of shadowy pines and spruces, lit by the chalk strokes of birch trunks and the vivid green of maples, and pierced by shafts of golden sunlight. The *shush ... shush ...* of wind through the canopy high above was as soothing as a hand stroking a cat's back.

But as they left the woods and started across the meadow toward the cottage, Cally's shoulders stiffened with tension.

When they rounded the cottage to the cliffward side Matthew appeared in the doorway. In one hand he held a steel tape measure, the tape extended like a blade. Noel halted a few paces from the door, hooked his thumbs in the belt of his chinos, and gazed back and forth along the building front. "How's it going? I don't see any signs of progress."

Matt raised the tape measure as a fencer puts up his foil. The tape snapped back into its case. "You wouldn't. All the work is inside."

"Weren't you going to do something about the roof, though?" Noel turned to Cally. "We found the place in bad shape this spring. Stones shifting, a lot of rot inside—"

"Not that much," Matt said.

Cally massaged one tight shoulder and tried to inject a cheery note. "I see you put a padlock on the door. Good idea!"

"Did it right after breakfast. I'd advise you all not to come too close. Some of those upper stones are loose."

Noel nodded thoughtfully. "You'll need a mason."

"Might do the job myself."

"I hope the floorboards are sound."

"They are."

Cally suddenly shivered. Noel shaped a smile, turned away and walked over to join the group near the edge of the cliff. Sheila was sitting cross-legged a pace back from the edge, looking out. As far as she could safely get from the cottage, Cally guessed. Ginevra had parked her wheelchair beside Sheila, and Aubrey sat on Gin's other side, with his feet sticking out over the edge. Having seen the cliff from the under side, Cally felt nervous watching all of them so close to that deadly drop.

Matthew sat down on the stone doorstep. Cally folded up onto the turf beside him, with her back to the wall. "Aren't you going to tell me this is a dangerous place to sit?"

"Because of the stones?" A corner of his mouth twitched. "Only one stone ever fell. Last year. The rest haven't moved in centuries."

"So you were just being your usual hospitable self. You're a lot like this cottage of yours, aren't you? All thick walls and narrow windows!"

"I'm really just a teddy bear." From a back pocket he brought out a flattened pack of cigarettes. "And don't say anything!"

"I wouldn't dream of it. They're your lungs, go ahead and destroy them."

He lit a cigarette and laid the burnt match carefully on the stone step beside him. He inhaled deeply, and his chest rose suddenly against the soft fabric of his sweatshirt.

Cally was aware of every movement he made, every shift of tone in his voice. His presence beside her had the impact of a thunderclap.

All her senses sharpened. The breeze brought a whiff of tobacco smoke, along with a slightly spicy, musky scent that might have been his sun-warmed skin. Mingled with it, the haylike smell of the grass she was pulling at. The tough, dry blades bit like wires into her fingers. Against her back the stones of the wall were cold. She sat forward to break the contact.

"I thought this place would be friendlier by day, but it isn't."

"It's a very old building, remember."

"Yes, but old buildings usually mellow. This one's gone bitter instead."

"You've got far too much imagination."

"Maybe. Anyway he must have been some determined character, whoever built it."

"You're right." Matt's eyes brightened. "My guess is he was an ex-army engineer. He would've had to bring his lime, for the mortar, up from Montreal. Same for his bolts and hinges and nails. Canoe most of the way, with several long portages. Not an easy trip."

"And glass for the windows? That must've been tricky."

His eyebrows flicked up. "You're joking, right?"

"Not glass?"

"Not here, not in those days. He glazed with mica sheets. I've found traces in the frames. Everything else he needed was on the spot. Lumber, clay and sand for the mortar, plenty of loose granite. And a Huron village close by if he needed extra hands, which he undoubtedly did."

"I hope he paid them!"

"If he did it was in goods, not coin. Blankets. Cooking pots. Knives. Anything made of steel would have been precious."

Cally couldn't resist keeping the conversation going. She enjoyed seeing his tight face relax and grow animated. It was obvious he loved this place.

"But why build here, in the middle of nowhere?"

He shot her a look of amusement. "Watch out, we're approaching that horrible story Sheila hates so much."

"I can take it," she said airily. "Gore doesn't bother me."

"Oh yeah?" He looked skeptical. "Well, here goes. My theory is that our guy was in hiding. He must have done something pretty bad, to make such an enemy. I think he was tired of running, and he built this place for a final battle, a showdown. Not that it did him any good in the end. You know what happened."

"He was killed along with the Hurons." Her fingers tightened on a handful of grass.

"Yup. It happened right here." He waved his cigarette at the grassy space in front of them. "Those that weren't killed outright were driven off the cliff."

Cally stared at the spread of yellow-green turf and the soft blue distance beyond. For a moment she thought she heard faint sounds: shouts, screams, the thud of running feet, all muted, like something happening very far away. Then there was only the swish of water on rocks and the cry of a gull. She wondered if the engineer had barricaded himself inside the cottage, and if so, how long he'd held out. She shook off a shudder.

Rising to her feet, she noticed for the first time a wooden rectangle propped slantwise against the side of the cottage, topping a low boxlike structure. "That's a cellar door, right? Could that be where our ghost hid last night?"

"No, that's been locked for a few years now. In any case the cellar's pretty shallow, only about two feet deep." He crushed out his cigarette on the doorstep and stood up.

"What's this about a ghost?" Noel strolled back, with Sheila trailing reluctantly behind him and Aubrey shepherding Gin's wheelchair.

"No ghost, just the usual inept vandals. Or vandal," Matt added dryly. He made a brief story of last night's expedition. The bald facts sounded more foolish than chilling.

"I must say you behaved rather irresponsibly." Noel was at his primmest. "Dragging Cally up here like that. You're lucky she wasn't hurt."

"I wasn't dragged," Cally objected. "I came off my own bat."

"That's right. Besides, what danger could there be?" Matt lit another cigarette, narrowing his eyes against the smoke. "Ghosts? Village kids? A startled rabbit?"

Noel answered soberly, "There's always a risk near these cliffs, you know that. Especially in the dark."

Ginevra piped up, "I can show Cally the spot where I had my accident." She swivelled her chair and pointed south. "Right over there. That's where I was standing when—" She broke off dramatically, then whispered, *"When I was pushed!"*

Cally shuddered. Then caught a mischievous gleam in Ginny's eye. "Ha! You almost got me."

"Actually it's true, I *was*—"

"Gin, will you shut up!" Sheila snapped. "Noel's right, Cally. That edge is dangerous. You must never go too close. It could crumble under you, and down you'd go."

They walked close to the edge, but not too close. Sheila held Noel's arm. Cally tried to peer over, but all she could see was some jutting bits of the giant's face — plane of cheekbone, tip of nose — and nothing of the undercut lower part of the cliff.

"It's at least two hundred feet down, and hard rock at the bottom," Noel said.

"I slid," Ginevra said importantly. "Right down the giant's face, but not off. I could've been killed but I wasn't."

"No thanks to common sense," Noel said.

"Great view, though," Cally put in. "Nothing but water and islands for miles and miles." But she shivered again. The whole cliff top, not just the cottage, breathed a hostile atmosphere. A dizzy feeling swam over her. The ground tilted under her feet. She took a quick step forward to regain her balance. A hand grabbed her arm and jerked her away from the brink.

She shrank back, cold and sick. The hand still gripped her arm. "Vertigo?" Matt murmured in her ear. She shook her head. This was a new thing: heights didn't bother her, or never had before. But a feeling stayed with her, bizarre as it sounded even to herself, that the island had just ducked its stony head and tried to tip her off into the void. And might have succeeded if Matt hadn't grabbed her.

Nobody else seemed to have noticed. But the air crackled with tension.

Sheila abruptly rounded on Matthew. "You shouldn't be smoking here! We agreed on that."

"Not in the woods, we said. Safe enough here."

"It is not safe! There are shrubs down on the shore. And look at the grass, it's like paper. All it needs is a bit of hot ash and we've got a fire!"

"Don't fuss. I'm always very careful." He flicked away the butt of his cigarette, watching as the wind carried it out on a long curve westward. The speck of white hit the water and was lost. Then he walked back to the cottage and in, closing the door after him.

Noel drew Sheila's arm through the crook of his elbow and patted her hand. She took a deep breath. "I'm sorry. I should have kept my mouth shut."

"Is there really a fire hazard?" Cally fell into step beside the twins as they started back across the meadow. Ginevra came behind, the big wheels of her chair bumping over the uneven turf, indignantly refusing Aubrey's help.

"Definitely." Noel snuffled the air. "Can't you smell the dryness? That wet weather we had in Toronto missed this region entirely. We need a good drenching."

"But surely Matthew wouldn't be careless about fire?"

"I never know what he might or might not do. But I think...." He hesitated. "Cally, I don't want to be interfering, but — watch your step, will you?"

"Around that cliff? You bet I will!"

"I don't mean the cliff. I mean Matthew."

She looked at him in surprise. "Are you going to decode that?"

"No," said Noel in his gentle, stubborn way. "We'll leave it at that. Just be careful. Oh, and one other thing. Last night I checked your door and found it wasn't locked. I'd advise you to keep it locked after this, at least by night. Better safe than sorry."

Chapter 7

CALLY SPENT MOST of the rest of the afternoon organizing her lesson plan for Ginevra. She sat at a little table on her balcony with a glass of iced tea at hand. The lessons would have to be appealing, intriguing and fun. It was going to be a titanic struggle to persuade the girl to concentrate on books in this paradise of summer.

Everyone came to dinner except, again, Matthew. The meal was subdued, despite Noel's determined attempts at conversation. Sheila seemed to lose her appetite almost immediately and sat pale and silent, sipping wine. Cally watched her worriedly and thought about the scene that afternoon on the cliff top. Aubrey and Ginevra between them started a few sparks of humour flying, but the sparks soon fizzled.

Ginevra buzzed away to the parlour early, pleading a desperate need to practice. Cally escaped soon after. She'd meant to go straight out the front door to the terrace, but a glance through the parlour door in passing pulled her to a halt. Ginevra was in there playing the piano. A man stood silhouetted against one of the windows, his back turned, hands in pockets. A visitor, Cally thought, someone fresh up from Toronto: there was something crisp and polished in his outline that said 'city'."

Then he turned his head, and it was Matthew. He had put on a light beige suit and a white shirt, open at the collar, that emphasized the tan of his face and neck. A scrubbed scent clung about him, and his thick dark hair, still damp, was neatly brushed back. And he had shaved. The change from scruffy to immaculate was riveting.

Cally was suddenly aware she was staring. Ginevra, who had stopped playing, grinned impishly over her shoulder. "Me and Matt are the pretty ones in the family."

He tousled her hair and smiled at Cally. "You see? I can make an effort, when I want to."

Cally grinned back. "You do clean up real nice!"

Noel came into the room then, arm in arm with Sheila, Aubrey sauntering behind. Cally expected Matt to move on, but he stayed. Never settled, though. He prowled restlessly about the room like a caged tiger (the thought sprang to her mind), picking up and putting down this or that gewgaw of porcelain or glass. He was so obviously out of sorts and out of place in this over-decorated room that she wondered what kept him there.

Noel paid him no attention, instead seeming to be absorbed in Aubrey's game of cribbage with Sheila. When the game was over Ginevra demanded Aubrey join her for a four-handed performance on the piano. Aubrey, who had been skunked, shouted, "No! I will have my revenge!" And they started a second game. Sheila had brightened up even though, to Cally's certain knowledge, she didn't care for card games.

Ginevra grumbled, then hoisted herself from the piano bench to her wheelchair and rolled over to where Cally was sitting by the window, looking out. "You haven't had the picture tour, have you?"

"Picture tour?"

"Yes! We always show people the pictures on this floor, especially in the library. Come on, I'm bored!"

"You can show me too." Matt turned from his study of a crystal swan and joined them.

"But you've already seen them."

"True, but I'm as bored as you are. Let's go!"

Ginevra was delighted to have doubled her audience. She buzzed ahead of them along the hall and into the dining room, where she briskly pointed out a series of watercolour landscapes: water, rocks, trees, simply rendered yet powerfully alive.

Peering, Cally could just make out the initials SF, very thin and tiny, half-hidden in a corner of each. "These are Sheila's. Aren't they great?"

"Come on!" Ginevra was beckoning impatiently from the double doors that led from the dining room to the library. Once inside, the wheelchair rolled straight through the library to the far end, where a large portrait hung over the fireplace. It wasn't hard to guess that this was the true object of the tour.

"Daddy had that done right after they were married. Of course the real good one is in our house in town. This is just a watercolour. But look: doesn't she just *shine* out of it?" Ginevra folded her arms and sat back as if prepared to gaze for the next hour.

"That she does," Matt said quietly. Cally glanced at his face and then away, feeling as if she were trespassing on private territory. Some deep sadness carefully packed away under layers of assumed indifference, that was what she saw, but didn't pretend to understand.

The picture was worth a long look, Cally had to agree. Ginevra's mother had been a breathtakingly beautiful woman. She strikingly resembled her daughter, although Gin was fairer.

"She's lovely, Gin! I can see why you wanted to show me this."

Ginevra's smile was misty. "She was musically gifted, too. But her life was cut tragically short. She died when I was just five, did you know that?"

The misty look vanished like fog in the sun when they passed to a picture on the right of the fireplace. It was George Forrest's first wife, Julia. She must have been about thirty when it was done, years before her death from cancer. Not a pretty woman, despite the clear blue eyes and regular features, but there was intelligence and decision in her face.

"I can see the resemblance to Noel," Cally said. "Not so much to Sheila."

"And I really like this one," Ginevra said, rolling around the room to a painting on the wall opposite the windows. "Even though it makes him look ugly."

"So do I." Matt walked over and stood studying a portrait done in pastels. "This is Sheila's work, unlike the other two, and in my opinion the best of the lot. She did this just three years ago."

George Forrest at sixty had been a big, bony, grizzled man with strong features. "I wouldn't say it makes him look ugly," Cally said. "She's shown his honesty and his strength. And his good nature. He looks like a man at peace with his world."

You could tell that the artist had loved her subject. Cally could also see a resemblance to Sheila in the set of the mouth and eyes. Something else in the pictured face looked familiar, but she couldn't pin it down, and then it was gone.

"And here's the last one! Sheila did this one too." Ginevra rolled ahead of them to the wall beside the door, where a medium-sized watercolour hung. This was a young woman, ash-blond, slim, chic. "That's Vanessa. She was Noel's girlfriend, years ago. I don't remember her much. But don't you think she looks just like a ferret?" She giggled.

Cally swallowed a laugh. There really was something weaselly in the refined lines of the nose and chin. "Is it a good likeness, Matt?"

"More of a caricature. Sheila has a gift for capturing the essence of a personality." His tone was dry and he barely glanced at the picture. It came to Cally that he had disliked this Vanessa.

"It's strange, isn't it, when you think— " Ginevra broke off and gazed wide-eyed around the room. "When you think what happened to them all. It's actually creepy! I mean, Julia, and my mother, and Vanessa...."

Matt stuck his hands in his pockets. "Don't start that again!"

"But it's true! Julia died of cancer, but she died awful young. And my mother fell from the cliff. And then Vanessa vanished from the island *just like that!* It's like we're really cursed! And me, I—"

"Ginny, stop!" He knelt before the wheelchair and gripped the armrests so she couldn't roll away. She gazed at him, her eyes huge pools of emotion. Cally couldn't make out whether Ginevra was really upset or whether she was acting out a spine-chilling drama.

"Listen to me!" Matt's voice was deep and calm. "You've got to stop manufacturing horrors. You're not just upsetting yourself, you're upsetting other people too. And for what?"

"But Julia—"

"Forget Julia. And forget Vanessa, she just got tired of Noel and walked away."

"But I—"

"Stop trying to create sinister patterns where there aren't any, you hear? I know it's tempting when life seems short on excitement, but it does nobody any good." He gave the chair a little shake.

Ginevra gazed at him a moment longer, then relaxed into a sigh. "Okay. I'll try."

"Good girl!" He got up and let go of the wheelchair.

"But, Matt?" Ginevra said in a small voice.

"Yes, kidlet?"

"You said forget Julia and Vanessa, but that still leaves my mother and me, right?" She looked up at him, and Cally could have sworn there was no play-acting going on now.

55

"Yes, but your mother—"

"She fell."

"I know." His mouth flattened.

"And I fell in the exact same place. And I don't care what anybody says, I was *pushed*!" Ginevra whirled her chair around and buzzed out of the room.

Matt grabbed his hair and tugged. "That kid! Someday the world will gain a great actress — if she doesn't get herself murdered first!"

Cally flinched. "I wish you wouldn't say 'murder' in connection with Ginevra."

He threw his hands up. "She drives me crazy! Even when she's being sincere she can't help delivering those scene-stealing exit lines."

"So she really thinks she was pushed? I suppose there's nothing in it?"

He glanced at her and away, frowning. Then back at her, scowling and intent. "There's something you should know. You'll hear it anyway, if you stay here. Especially if you spend much time in the village. The locals think one of us did it. Some say it was me, some say it was Sheila."

"What! But that's stupid!"

"I agree, but that's what they think. Mrs. Gardner won't spill it, but some others might. The idea is that it goes back to Francesca marrying our dad. Sheila never really forgave him for it, I know that for sure. You see, after Julia died, Sheila became Dad's best little helper and pal. She loved him and she loved being the lady of the house." Matt shook his head at the memory.

"Then along came Francesca." Cally looked up at the glowing portrait over the fireplace.

"Right. And Dad was blown away. I'd never seen him so happy!"

He smiled up at the portrait. "She was so beautiful, so warm, so full of life! And poor Sheila ... well, there she was on the margin again. Not Dad's best girl any more. Hardly noticed, sometimes."

"Poor Sheila!"

"Yeah. And it was obvious how she felt about that. Sheila was never good at hiding her feelings. So that summer when Francesca fell from the cliff, that's when the talk started."

"Wait, you don't mean they said—"

"That Sheila pushed Francesca off the cliff out of jealousy."

"But Sheila was only — what, seventeen then? Sixteen?"

"Eighteen. And later, as Gin got older and claimed more of Dad's attention, she tried to get rid of Francesca's daughter too. So they say."

In the cold silence that followed, Cally pictured a red-haired little girl poised on the edge of a cliff. And someone stepping silently up behind her. A shove, a scream, and she was gone.

"Look here!" She turned fiercely on Matt. "Ten to one Gin fell by accident, then made up that story to make herself important. She's that kind of kid, right?"

"Maybe, but—"

"Because nobody, *nobody* would push a child off a cliff just out of spite. I won't believe it!"

"Take it easy, Cally. I don't want to believe it either. And I know for a fact Sheila didn't push Francesca. But don't stick your head in the sand, eh? There's a lot of spite in somebody around here."

He crossed to the portrait over the fireplace and gazed up at it for a long moment, then turned back to meet Cally's searching eyes. Something still glowed in his face, like a reflection of the portrait's golden tones. It occurred to her that he hadn't explained why some people thought he might be the guilty one. And how did he know "for a fact" Sheila wasn't?

"And you?" she asked. "What did you think of Francesca?"

"Me?" The glow faded. Now he looked grim and distant. She knew she wasn't going to get an answer.

"You cared about her, didn't you?"

He snapped back to the here and now. His eyes narrowed. "Why should I bother telling you anything? Why don't you just read what's written on my forehead?"

"Keep out of my skull — that's what it says."

"Good advice. Because you won't always like what you'll find in there." He circled around her and walked out the door.

Cally felt dull and chilled, as if a light inside had gone out. She went back to the parlour, where she played three-handed cribbage for another hour, and tried to persuade herself that she didn't give a rat's ass what Matthew Forrest thought of her or who he'd ever cared about.

Chapter 8

ON SUNDAY MORNING Cally came downstairs late again, to find Sheila alone in the breakfast room. She loaded a plateful of scrambled eggs, ham and toast and sat down at the table.

Sheila leaned against the sideboard, nursing a cup of coffee. "Not going to church?"

"Uh-oh. Was I expected to?"

"Not really. Dad never missed a Sunday, so now Noel 'keeps up the tradition,' as he puts it. There he goes now."

Through the sliding glass door Cally watched an oddly assorted group trooping along the path to the pier. Noel led the way, and even at this distance she could admire the cut of his pearl-grey suit and the gleam of his white oxfords. Ginevra's wheelchair rolled along behind him. By the sullen hunch of Gin's shoulders you could tell that going to church was not at all her idea. Next marched a short, sturdy, sixtyish woman in a flowered polyester dress and beribboned summer hat: Mrs. Gardner, the cook. At her heels came Edna, her thin little teenaged helper, in a T-shirt and denim skirt that were both too big for her.

Cally watched them disappear down the hill, then turned from the window. "Where's everybody else?"

"Well, Aubrey — you can hear where he is." Sheila cupped her ear toward the sound of the piano in the next room. "And Jack's out there dividing the irises — actually working, for a change."

"Ah." Cally munched toast.

"What you really mean is *Where is Matt.* Right?"

"Don't be silly!" But her thrice-cursed flush was acting up again. She could feel its betraying heat creeping up her neck.

"He's gone to the cottage, as usual. Not expected back for dinner. Took sandwiches and a cooler of water and beer with him, Mrs. Gardner said. You see, I like to keep track of him too."

Cally set down her toast and gave Sheila a straight look. "In your way, you're as silly about Matt as I am."

Sheila shook her head. "Not silly. Careful." She drained her coffee and went out.

So: Matt was gone for the day. Cally expected to see little of him from now on. Yesterday he had opened up more than once and shown her a glimpse of the man he was inside. People usually did regret such spur-of-the-moment intimacies, especially people who habitually kept their feelings to themselves.

Never mind, she told herself. Forget him. Enjoy this perfect summer day.

THEY SPENT MOST of the day outdoors. They swam. They played croquet, Ginevra too. They sunned themselves and drank tall glasses of iced water and juice, and talked back and forth in lazy voices.

As the sun sank Sheila and Cally went up to wash and change for dinner. Noel wanted them all to dress up a bit more than usual, seeing it was Sunday, which Cally thought was almost too quaintly old-fashioned even for him. She put on her best dress, a long white silky gauze wrapped at the waist and shot through with gold threads. Her hair was too short to do anything fancy with, so she pulled it back over one ear with a gold clip and told her mirror that would have to do.

Normally, despite Noel's pretentions, she would have loved dressing up. There was always the fun of play-acting, pretending to be someone else, someone rich and beautiful and self-assured. But tonight she couldn't work up much enthusiasm for the masquerade.

Why? Because Matt won't be there? Cally, you're not that big a fool!

THE LINGERING CHORDS of *Stardust* drifted through the open parlour windows. Cally sat entranced in the dusk. A breeze pressed the silk of her dress against her leg and lifted a stray strand of hair to tickle her nose. The fragrance of night-blooming nicotiana came with it.

The dancers floated across the dark lawn. Sheila had taken pains with her appearance. She swayed in a swath of lavender taffeta and her fine dark hair was let loose to flow after her. Noel in his formal black clothes was shiningly fair and boyish. They moved together so harmoniously that you remembered they were twins, closer than the average brother and sister.

The music ebbed into silence. "Tell them to keep playing!" Noel called. Cally went inside to pass on the message.

"If he thinks I'm going to sweat over a hot piano just so he can hog all the women!" Aubrey slid off the piano bench and knelt to pull CDs out of the stereo cabinet. "*Big Bands ... Summer Songs ... Moonlight and Roses....*"

"Bleh!" Ginevra, nearby in her wheelchair, held her nose.

"Oh, I know. Icky-sweet, but that's the stuff we want." He distributed CDs on the five-disk player and closed the lid. "And away they go! Come on, Gin, we're free at last!"

He got to his feet, straightening his white tie. He wore an ancient swallow-tailed tuxedo that looked all of its years and was a size too big for him. "My concert suit," he'd called it, straight-faced, when he appeared at dinner. Noel had dryly complimented him on possessing

61

"such a classic." Sheila had looked him over, flushed with laughter. Cally had rolled her eyes.

"How do I look?" he said now.

"Like a flea circus ringmaster."

"I think you look awesome!" Ginevra said. "I have to wear this yucky thing." She plucked at the too-small pink ruffled concoction she was wearing. "I asked Matt to take me shopping for new clothes before school starts, but he won't."

"That's not a job for a man, anyway. Ask Sheila, she'd be glad to take you."

"Phooey!" Ginevra made a face. "She's never any fun. Cally, you can take me, can't you? Say yes!"

"Well...."

"Please, please, pleeeease!"

"Well, okay, if Noel and Sheila agree."

"Yes!" She scooped up a copy of *Elle* and rolled out of the room and out the front door to the terrace. Aubrey folded Cally's hand into the crook of his elbow and walked her out with just slightly overdone dignity.

When they turned the corner of the house Cally took a quick breath and freed her arm. Then breezed on as if she was not in the least ruffled to find Matt there. He was sitting in the chair she had left, watching Noel and Sheila twirl across the lawn to the lush strains of a Strauss waltz. Ginevra had already swivelled her wheelchair into place on Matt's right.

Cally poured a glass of Chardonnay and held it out. He took it and lifted it in a wordless salute. Aubrey took the chair on Matt's left while Cally perched on the low stone balustrade that edged the terrace. It placed her a safe two yards away.

"You passed up the dinner of the century," she told him lightly.

"I didn't feel like getting gussied up. You've found out what Noel is like on a Sunday." He raised his arm to display a ragged hole in the elbow of his sweatshirt. "What did I miss?"

"Crown roast of lamb," Ginevra began eagerly, "tiny new potatoes, all crusty brown — I love those—"

Aubrey and Cally chimed in with more mouth-watering details. Matt laughed, sat up straight, and pushed the shaggy hair back from his forehead.

Extraordinary! Cally couldn't stop looking. It was as if he'd pulled off a mask to show another man's face: a happier, handsomer, younger man.

Aubrey leaped up, slipped an arm around her waist and pulled her from the balustrade. "Dance, my little one, dance!" he cried, and whirled her down the steps and across the lawn without waiting for an answer. Behind them Cally heard Ginevra's plaintive voice: "Oh, how I wish I could dance! And I never, ever will!"

"I got you away just in time," Aubrey said in Cally's ear. "You were ogling the man! I was embarrassed for you!"

"Don't be silly!"

"All he has to do is smile and you're all eyes. For shame!"

"Shush! Look at Matt. Look, he's going to dance with Ginny!"

Matt had lifted Ginevra in his arms and carefully descended the terrace steps. Now, slowly, gracefully, he circled across the lawn to the music of the Emperor Waltz. As he turned Cally saw his face, quiet and serene. Ginevra, her arms clasped about his neck, looked out with shining eyes.

Cally stood enchanted, and across the lawn Noel and Sheila watched, still and silent. "How beautiful," Cally murmured. "It's so obvious what's been wrong with him. If only they'd give him half a chance!"

"Not bloody likely," Aubrey said.

The still figures across the lawn suddenly came to life. Noel strode to intercept the dancers. Cally pushed Aubrey away, picked up her skirts and ran to join them.

"No, Matt, *now*." Noel's tone was final. "Sheila, bring the wheel-chair."

"But I want to dance!" Ginevra wailed.

"Matt might trip, and drop you, and you'd be hurt."

"No he wouldn't!"

"Let me be the judge, Ginny. It's very unwise of him. Here's the chair. Now, Matt. Put her down!"

Please God, Cally prayed, please don't let them start at each other again. She began, "Noel, I'm sure he can manage, and she's enjoying it so much—"

"Yes I am, and I want to dance — Noel, please!"

"Will you for once be *quiet!*" His voice was a whip. Ginevra shrank against Matt's shoulder. He held her more closely for a moment. Then, still silent, he bent and lowered her into the chair.

Ginevra clutched the arms of the chair, squeezed her eyes shut, threw back her head and let out a piercing shriek of rage. Then she was on the move, buzzing at top speed across the lawn and up the ramp to the terrace. She vanished into the house.

Matt turned to look straight at Noel. He had changed again, gone hard and dangerous.

Noel met his look with a lift of the chin. "Don't think I like to spoil her fun. But remember, I'm her guardian, not you. I'm respon-sible for the child. Suppose you'd fallen?"

"No chance of that." Matt's voice was velvety.

"That's for me to decide. Now, I feel I must warn you. You're not to place Ginevra at risk like that — or in any other way — ever again. Is that understood?" He sounded like a schoolteacher laying down the law to a dirty-faced delinquent.

Matt's features might have been carved in stone. Cally held her breath.

Then he turned from Noel, came face to face with Cally, and enfolded her in a dancer's embrace. The waltz still played. They moved through the spill of yellow light from the windows and on across the shadowy lawn, and it felt as normal yet fantastic as dancing in a dream. Cally was too much aware of his charged silence to say anything, too aware of his body brushing against hers to frame words.

"Thank God you were there," he muttered at last. "If you hadn't been, I might have slugged him. One of these days I will. He'll push me too far."

She put back her head to see his face. His eyes were hard and bright, reflecting the house lights. "Does he know he's doing that?" she asked. "Maybe he's just being Noel. You know how fussy he gets."

"He knew exactly what he was doing." His chest rose against her shoulder in a sigh. "And it's not what Dad wanted."

"Which is what, exactly?"

He spun her off to his fingertips, smiled at her from that distance, and let her go. "Did you never wonder why Dad left us the island in two parts? The top part to me, the bottom part with the house to Noel?"

"I assumed it was because you had an interest in the old cottage. As an architect, I mean."

"Yes, but it wasn't just that." He strolled back across the lawn, outwardly at ease, but he never took his eyes off the silhouetted figures on the terrace. "Dad, bless him, had the bright idea that if we had to share the island we'd learn to get along with each other. There are decisions that have to be made jointly. And this summer together? He put it in his will."

"You can will a thing like that?"

"No, of course he couldn't legally enforce it. But he did say it was the dearest wish of his heart — I'm quoting — that we spend time together on the island. That we learn to act like brothers." He stopped strolling. "You can see how well that's working out."

"I can't for the life of me understand what the problem is."

"It goes way back."

"Yes, and?"

"And anything I say will come across as self-serving. Ask Noel. Better yet, ask Sheila. Just try to keep an open mind. That's all I ask." He strode back to the house, crossed the terrace and on in, without a glance at the three sitting there.

Chapter 9

"WELL, THAT WAS some scene." Cally settled on the terrace balustrade facing Noel. "Poor Ginny!"

"Poor Ginny my foot!" Noel sniffed, half amused, half annoyed. "Ginny doesn't know what's best for her, and why should she? She's just a child. As her guardian, Cally, I do have to be careful."

"Careful about your own brother?"

Noel flipped a hand in a minimal shrug.

"Matt told me about why the island was divided between the two of you. He didn't explain why your father thought that was necessary." She added, "Of course it's none of my business."

It was full night now. The CD player still warbled softly, but the lamps in the parlour had been switched off to avoid attracting moths and mosquitoes. There was no moon, only stars, and the faint ghost-flames of the aurora licking up the sky from the north. The dark created an intimacy not possible in daylight. Facial expressions were invisible, tones of voice took on deeper meanings.

Sheila stirred, rustling her dress. "I'll say it, Noel, if you won't. And Cally, you're right, it is none of your business — only you've made yourself vulnerable, and there are things you should know."

"Vulnerable? What—"

"Just listen. You know Matt was adopted. Well, Mother never really accepted him. To be fair, she might even have neglected him."

"I never thought she did," Noel said. "She did her duty by him. She was that kind of person."

"Anyway, Dad more than made up for it, didn't he?"

"That's debatable. But I believe Matt did resent Mother's taking our part. And blamed me for it. I guess he still holds that against me, although you'd think, after all these years, he could let it go."

"He's like that," Sheila said. "Won't let things go. Won't let people go, either."

"Don't," Noel said quietly. "Please."

"She should know. Cally, this is about Vanessa."

Without another word Noel got up and went inside, closing the front door behind him. Cally glanced up at the house. Farther along this side, two yellow rectangles showed on the second floor: Matt's windows. She wondered if he could hear what they were saying.

Sheila followed her glance and rose with a whisper of taffeta. "Let's go for a walk." Aubrey jumped up. She shook her head at him. "Girl talk. No boys allowed." They left him staring after them and crossed the dark lawn to the beach path. On the pier the cool scent of the water rose around them, soothing as a caress.

Cally sat down on the end of the pier, pulled off her sandals, tucked up her long skirt and swished her feet in the water. She began to feel a degree less keyed-up.

"What's he been telling you?" Sheila asked quietly, sitting down beside her.

"Matt? Nothing much. Just that your father wanted his sons to act like brothers, and Noel isn't having any of it."

"Did you know Vanessa was Matt's girlfriend before she switched to Noel?"

"No. I didn't know."

"That was four years ago but Matt never forgot it, and he never forgave either of them."

An unhappy silence fell between them. It was a still night. Cally could hear every little sound: each wave lapping the beach, the stir and slosh of water against the piles under the pier. The lake stretched away from them into the invisible distance, huge and black and hungry.

Hungry. Why had she thought that?

She pulled her feet out of the lake, flicked water off them and tucked them under her skirt for warmth. All of her felt cold now, inside and out. "How did it happen?"

"Vanessa? She came to a party with Matt and left with Noel."

"Classy!"

"Really," Sheila said dryly. "Personally, I think it was Noel's prospects that she found so attractive. Matt was in a young architectural firm that was struggling then, while Noel was in line to be a partner in Dad's carpet import company, which was doing really well."

"Why would Noel want a woman like that?"

"He wouldn't, of course. He never believed she was that mercenary. To this day he's convinced Vanessa wanted out of a bad situation, and he was rescuing her. You see, Matt had gotten into an argument with the host, and he — Noel — reproached him for being disruptive, and Matt very rudely told him to keep his nose out of it. Then Vanessa, Noel says, backed him — Noel — up, and then Matt went into one of his terrible silent rages, the way he did tonight. So Noel took Vanessa away."

"Hm." Cally pulled up her knees and wrapped her arms around them. "She didn't stay with him long, did she?"

"No, and — Cally." Sheila's voice sounded stifled. "That was Matt's fault."

"What, he scared her away?" This didn't sound like the Matt she thought she was beginning to know. It sounded petty. "I'd have thought he'd have too much pride."

"All we know is, she was staying on the island that summer and one day she was just gone. No warning. She left a note for Noel and she'd packed her bags. One of the motorboats was found tied to the wharf at Blackwater Bay. We think she rented a car there."

"To where?"

"Noel had her traced as far as New York. After that, nothing."

"You mean he just let her go?" Cally was shocked.

"She was a free woman, she could go where she liked." Sheila shrugged. "He worried, but personally I think he was better off without her."

"But didn't it seem strange, her going off like that?"

"Cally, remember what I said about Matt. He doesn't let go." Sheila got up and shook out her skirts. "Maybe he tried to get her back. Maybe he pushed her too far. Maybe he threatened her. Maybe he—"

"No! I can't see him being so—"

"You don't know him, Cally!"

Cally climbed to her feet. She searched Sheila's face. "There's something more, isn't there? Something else you're not telling me."

"It's nothing you'd want to know. Don't ask me again."

"You won't be honest with me, yet you expect me to take your side?"

"I'm being as honest as I can. Cally, please! Don't let Matt do this to us. Don't let him drive us apart."

"Oh! Sheila, that'll never happen." Cally impulsively hugged her. "We'll always be friends. You should know nothing can change that."

They pulled on their sandals and climbed the path to the house. The windows on the second floor were still lit.

After Sheila had gone in Cally stood on the terrace, craving the peace of the quiet night. Her thoughts were whirling. This story about Vanessa and Matt, now. There was something unconvincing about it, something almost hysterical in Sheila's insistence that Matt was dangerous. And yet Sheila was not stupid or imperceptive, far from it. And she was no liar. If anything, she was too painfully honest.

Movement caught her eye and she looked up. A tall shadow crossed and recrossed Matt's windows. He was pacing like a caged animal.

Out of the turmoil one idea spun loose. She flinched as she examined it, tried to dismiss it, but it wouldn't go away. What was the very best reason for a person to vanish and never be heard from again? If that person were dead.

Chapter 10

ON MONDAY MORNING the weekday routine was established. Ginevra studied with Cally from nine to eleven-thirty, and then wheeled down to the beach to do swimming exercises with Sheila for an hour. Then came lunch, and after that Gin studied piano for as long as Aubrey would let her.

"I have a much better opinion of her talent now than I had last year," he said. "And her drive! The kid really wants to work at this."

"I wish I could say the same," Cally grumbled from where she lay stretched out near him on the hot grey timbers of the pier. "Oh, she'll get through the material. She's bright and she has a good memory, when she actually focuses. But when I ask for discussion she has nothing to say."

She stood up and poised on the edge of the pier, bracing herself for shock. These were not waters you could ease yourself into. You had to plunge in and get the worst over. But after one moment of icy hell it was heaven: clear as glass, here, for twelve feet to the sandy bottom, and shot through with quivering sunlight.

Without warning a hand clapped her thigh and shoved. She tumbled into the lake with a shriek and a flailing of arms and a moment later broke the surface, gasping and murderous. Aubrey chortled at her, then dove off the other side of the pier, inviting a chase. She shook her head and splashed over to the boathouse, five yards away. A narrow wooden walkway ran around the outside of the shed. She pulled herself up onto it and perched there, panting.

"Marvellous," she murmured. In this golden noon all night fears and rumours of violence seemed laughable. Across the stretch of ruffled blue water she made out the dark speck and flash of white that was Sheila returning. Sheila was a strong swimmer, although to look at her you'd never guess it. Her daily routine was to swim to an islet half a mile to the south, and back. Her only problem was staying clear of powerboats.

Ginevra, meanwhile, sat forlornly on the end of the pier with her feet dangling over the water. Her bare legs were pitifully thin and white; but not, Cally thought, wasted, even though she made a big fuss about exercising. Cally couldn't make out whether Ginny was making an effort in these sessions or not. It looked as if Sheila was doing all the work, yet Ginevra seemed to become exhausted. When Aubrey lifted her out onto the pier she had to sit wrapped in a big towel, shivering wretchedly.

Aubrey laughed at her. "All dramatics! Anybody'd think you didn't want to get better."

Cally had privately asked Sheila if there was a possibility that Ginevra would ever walk again.

"Yes, there is a chance, a small one. The doctors say the nerves in her spine were damaged, but not irreversibly. There's no organic reason why she can't start regaining at least some muscle function."

"Then why doesn't she?"

"We don't know. But somewhere there's something that keeps her brain from sending a message to her legs. We'll just have to keep trying."

CALLY PUSHED OPEN the boathouse door and spotted a craft the shape and colour of a pea pod lying on a ledge, its paddles nearby. She slid the canoe into the water, then carefully lowered herself until she was sitting, more or less comfortably, in what she believed was the correct position. She picked up a paddle, dipped it into the water and glided out into the sunshine.

Then dug the paddle in and halted the canoe as Sheila crossed her path, arms rhythmically rising and reaching. They met at the outer end of the pier, well away from where Ginevra and Aubrey sat in the shallows close to the beach, battling with water pistols.

"Get run over today?"

"One just missed me this time." Sheila trod water and pushed dark strands away from her face. "Then the idiots thought I was drowning and tried to pull me into their stupid boat!" Water streaming off her, she climbed onto the pier and reached for her towel. "I see you found Matt's canoe. I hope you asked his permission."

"No, I didn't. Didn't know it was his. Will he mind?"

"I never know how he'll react to anything." Sheila towelled her hair vigorously. She turned toward the house, and froze.

A shadow fell across the canoe. Cally looked up, shading her eyes. Matthew was a black shape looming between her and the sun. It was impossible to make out his expression.

"I hope you don't mind my borrowing your canoe," she said in a formal tone. "I didn't know it was yours until just now."

"I don't mind, so long as you handle it properly. And don't take it out any distance. It's obvious you have no experience." He was cool and neutral.

"Obvious? How?" She was nettled. "I thought I was doing fine."

"You're not. For starters, you're sitting all wrong. Your feet shouldn't stick out in front like that. You should have your knees down and your feet tucked under the thwart."

"Thwart?"

"That thing you're sitting on."

"Oh." She rearranged her legs, pulling forward a foam cushion for her knees.

"Now, the way you're holding that paddle—" He made a sound of disgust. "Come around here so I can show you."

Cally tried to paddle around the end of the pier, but the canoe, so docile before, now turned balky and refused to go where she pointed it. Finally she put the paddle down and used her hands to move the canoe along the length of the pier toward the shallows. Aubrey and Ginevra had launched model warships and were manoeuvring them with blasts from the water pistols.

At the six-foot depth Matt said, "Far enough." He lay down on the planks so he could grasp the gunwale with one down-stretched hand. His face was disturbingly close above hers, every detail spotlit by the dancing light reflected from the surface of the water. He needed a shave again. His clear grey eyes had taken on a tinge of blue from the lake. The framing lashes were short, thick and black.

Cally was disoriented. She was swimming underwater, the rest of the world shut out behind walls of silvery blue. The moment stretched out....

The moment passed. She was sitting in the canoe with the sun flashing into her eyes. At the same moment she recalled that this was a man who was said to have frightened a woman so badly that she ran away and got herself untraceably lost.

"All right," he said briskly. "Pick up the paddle. Left hand over the butt. Your right hand's too high, slide it down. Okay: now, dip in — no, not like that!"

"What?"

"You're not trying to spear fish! Sit up straight, don't lean forward. Now dip in. *Push* with your butt hand. *Pull* with the other. Is this the first time you've done this?"

"Certainly not," she said with dignity. "I rented a canoe on the

Avon River once, with a friend. At Stratford."

"Oh, yeah." He grinned. "Dangerous waters."

"Seriously, it was risky. Those swans can be vicious."

He let out a snort of laughter.

Sheila, who had decided not to go up to the house, made a *tch!* of disgust. "Look who's coming. And even from here you can tell he's drunk as a skunk."

Ducking her head to look under the pier, Cally saw the big red powerboat curving across the lake toward them. A wide wobble marred its course. Next moment she knew it was coming on too fast.

Aubrey scrambled up with Ginevra in his arms and backed onto the sand. Matt rose to his knees, yelling "Cut the engine!" Jack shut off the motor, but too late. He looked set to crash into the pier.

At the last possible moment he swerved. Straight for Cally. She stared, frozen, at the huge red shape that plowed toward her, an image that held still between one stumbling heartbeat and the next.

Then she was caught up into the air and the powerboat bit into the canoe with a sickening crunch. Jack, who had risen into a half-crouch, flew over the side and landed with an enormous splash in two feet of water. There he lay thrashing and choking, and working himself in deeper.

Cally went limp. Matt still held her braced against his body as they knelt together on the pier. The rise and fall of his chest against her shoulder was wonderfully comforting. A chill swept through her, then a wave of radiant warmth: aftermath of shock, she guessed. She saw no reason to end the embrace, not when it felt so right, so healing and yet exhilarating.

Then Matt said, "Jack's in trouble," and took his arms away. He stood up and jumped off the pier. After a dazed moment she jumped in after him and together, each grasping a flailing arm, they hauled

Jack onto the beach. He fought them all the way.

By then Aubrey had carried Ginevra to her wheelchair and Sheila was at the water's edge. She took Cally by the shoulders and looked her over anxiously. "Are you all right?"

"Well, you saw." She still felt trembly in the knees. "Matt rescued me. I'm fine."

"He could have killed her!" Matt burst out. He stared down in disgust at the human wreck stirring at his feet. "Sheila, you've got to get rid of him. He's a disaster!"

"I agree," she said crisply. "But don't tell me, tell Noel. He's the one who pays him."

Jack sat up and raised one shaking hand. "So I take a d- dr- a dink. Mis'r Noel don't mind."

"You could have crushed Cally to death! By God, I ought to—" Matt made a fist. Jack staggered upright and made for the path at top speed.

"Lunchtime!" Ginevra called over her shoulder, as she wheeled slowly up the looping hill path, with Aubrey close behind.

Sheila caught Cally's hand. "Coming?"

"In just a sec."

Sheila hesitated, then followed the others.

Cally found Matthew at the water's edge, hands on the hips of his soaked jeans, scowling at the now submerged canoe. Seeing that the powerboat was floating free, she caught it just before it drifted out of reach and tied it to one of the steel rings on the side of the pier.

Meanwhile, Matt waded into the water and hauled the canoe onto the beach. There he turned it over and let the water pour out. On one side the green fibreglass was caved in around a star-shaped cluster of cracks.

"Is it ruined?"

He knelt in the sand and bent close to study the damage. "Probably not. I may be able to fix this myself." He no longer sounded angry. Instead he was treating her like a casual bystander, not looking at her, sending his remarks into the air.

She walked around to the other side of the canoe and knelt facing him.

"You still here?" He glanced at her vaguely. "Isn't your lunch waiting?"

"Can't I help?"

"Don't see how, unless you have a resin kit stashed in that swimsuit. No, eh? I'll have to go to the village."

She tried again, softly. "You saved my life."

He didn't answer. Surely he'd been over every square inch of that damaged surface by now, but he kept on scanning it and poking at it.

"Thank you for—"

"Forget it. See you later, maybe." He got to his feet and turned away.

"Matt, wait!"

He stopped, but didn't face her.

"You heard, didn't you? Last night. What we were saying. About Vanessa."

"Some." He turned and looked at her coolly. "Enough to guess the rest."

"Then deny it, why not? Or explain it!"

"I can't explain what I don't know myself."

"I don't understand. Why—"

"Like I said before. Just keep an open mind." He walked away toward the pier.

Chapter 11

BY MID-AFTERNOON the heat had driven everyone indoors to shaded rooms, ceiling fans, and iced drinks. Cally's head was aching. Not surprising, after that crisis by the pier. She went to her room, closed the drapes against the tide of sunshine, found a sleep mask and lay down on top of the covers.

Sleep would not come. Questions buzzed inside her head. Jack Beamish, for one. How on earth did he keep his job when, it seemed, he was never more than half sober? Surely, after what happened to-day....

And Sheila: why did she fear Matt so? Dislike, yes, that was understandable. But fear? And what dire secret was she nursing? Because there was something she wasn't sharing, that was certain.

And Ginevra: Was she pushed, that time she fell from the cliff? Or did she imagine it? She wasn't lying, anyway: she seemed to really believe it. Could Sheila have.... No, absolutely not!

Cally turned over and searched for a cool spot on the pillow. Her head was throbbing worse than ever.

And Matthew. Matt, the walking question mark. What had he seen when he looked up at that portrait of Gin's mother? Francesca had mattered, one way or another. Still mattered. And his affection for Gin: was that for Francesca's sake? What had they been to each other? And why wouldn't he say, plain and simple, just what had passed between him and Vanessa on the island, the summer she disappeared?

Images floated across her inner vision. Sheila's paintings, printed behind her eyelids as if they hung on a gallery wall. Especially that picture of Matt on the cliff. It haunted her: the threat of a gathering storm, the sense of menace poised to turn on the viewer. And the incongruous, significant playing card in the back pocket. Ace of spades. That meant something bad, didn't it? Some dangerous power. Bad luck. Death.

Cally slept fitfully, pursued by broken dreams.

NO ONE ENJOYED DINNER much. Ginevra complained of the heat and Sheila was irritably silent. Noel, who had spent much of the day in Port Devon tending to business long-distance, was preoccupied with the danger of fire. "You hear talk of it everywhere. In the coffee shop, in the stores, at the marina. There are fires all over the region, some not so far from here."

"But we're on an island," Aubrey pointed out with an air of discovery. "There's water on all sides of us. Why should we worry?"

"Because lightning could start a fire anywhere. And because we don't have the means to get enough water from the lake to the fire. We only have the two small extinguishers in the house, and a couple of garden hoses."

"We should put in a better pump," Sheila said. "Remember we told Dad so, a couple of years ago?"

"And he vetoed it. Said it cost too much." Noel laughed softly. "Always a bit tight with the purse strings, Dad was. But yes, you're right, and I'll look into it. Meantime, I want you all to remember, absolutely no barbecues, campfires or smoking in or near the woods."

THE SUN WAS a red flare behind the treetops. You could almost see it sink, see the blue tide of dusk creep up the white wall. The air was languorously warm.

Around the corner of the house, the front door opened and Ginevra's wheelchair buzzed out and along the terrace, stopping beside Cally's canvas chair.

"You asleep?"

"No."

"You sick?"

"No."

"Here, then." Papers plopped down on Cally's lap, and the wheelchair buzzed off.

The papers were a two-page hand-written essay on Masefield's poem *Cargoes*, the result of that morning's assignment. Cally found it well-organized, correctly spelled, and entirely without originality.

She hiked her yellow cotton dress above the knees and slipped off her sandals to feel the almost-cool flagstones under her bare feet. Ginny was playing the piano now, a frail plinking sound that barely held its own against the urgent trilling of the crickets. The voices through the parlour window seemed to come from very far away. The sun flickered behind the woods and then was gone, leaving behind a deep rose-coloured sky like a sunburn.

The evening held its breath. Not a leaf stirred. Cally found her nerves more keyed up than ever.

It must be the weather. Something's ... got ... to break....

In her next conscious moment she was sitting bolt upright and gazing up into Matt's eyes. He was bent over, a hand on each arm of her chair, examining her.

He straightened up. He had showered, shaved and put on fresh jeans and a clean denim shirt. "Funny place to sleep," he said. "Something wrong with you?"

"I had a headache, but I'm fine now." She rubbed her temples. "All I need is something cold to drink." He bent, picked a clinking glass up off the flagstones and held it out. She smiled at him, and was glad to see a hint of a smile in return.

"Thanks." She took the glass and held it against her cheek. Its icy wetness woke her fully. He sat down in the chair to her right and held his own glass on his knee. They looked out over the garden, blue now with twilight under the trees, ruddy in the open areas under the glowing sky.

"How's the canoe?"

"Fixed. You can use it tomorrow if you want."

"You'd trust me with it?"

"You need more practice with the paddle, but yeah."

"Thanks."

"It's a peace offering."

She shot a surprised look at him sideways. "For what, being Mr. Grumpy today?"

"I think the usual title is Surly Bastard."

She laughed. "Well, if you can play nice, so can I. I promise I won't go talking out of turn again."

"I don't want you to promise that. Go ahead and say what you like. It does me good. And ask what you like. I may or may not answer, but feel free."

She gave up on subtlety, turned in her chair and stared. He hadn't looked at her once since sitting down and he didn't now. He swallowed the last of his drink, then turned the slippery glass around in his fingers.

"Truth is," he said to the glass, "something's happening, and I don't like it. I was hoping we could make a new start this summer — Noel and me — for Dad's sake. But it's no go. There's a wall there, and something else. Something's wrong, and I just can't pin it down." The glass turned round and round. "But I had no right taking out my worries on you."

Unless he was an Oscar-calibre actor, he was telling the truth: at least, the truth as he saw it. It rang in his voice. And it left her with one very large problem. Those things Sheila had said about him. He still hadn't tried to defend himself. Ask me anything, he'd said. Okay, so now was the time.

She opened her mouth to speak but at that moment came the sound of the front door opening and then Sheila strolled around the corner of the house arm in arm with Noel. Her face was a pale oval in the dusk: too pale, Cally thought. But Noel was smiling, radiating good cheer. Ginevra buzzed out after them and Aubrey brought up the rear, a sweating bottle of beer in his hand. Matt got up and moved back one of the empty chairs so Ginny could park beside him. The others sat down in a row next to Cally, with Noel on her left.

The garden was dark now, softly lit by a slim crescent moon and a citronella candle that flickered in a jar on the balustrade. The parlour drapes were closed. Ice clinked in glasses.

"I'm bored," Ginny announced. "Let's play a game."

"Perhaps later." Noel cleared his throat. "I phoned our lawyer today," he announced.

Sheila said, "About?"

"About the divided ownership of the island. I asked whether there might be some legal means of forcing a sale of one portion or the other. He said not."

Matt's glass squeaked as his fingers gripped. Cally's nerves ratcheted tighter.

"But why," Sheila began, then let it go.

"I've already asked Matt twice to sell me his end of the island. He's refused twice. I propose right now to ask him a third time. Matt—"

83

"Same answer."

Silence fell like lead. Cally wondered why her heart was thumping so. A disagreement about real estate, for heaven's sake!

But it wasn't just that. *Something's happening.* "Um, Noel, if you don't mind my asking?"

"Go ahead, Cally, by all means."

"Why is it so important for you to own both parts of the island? Why can't you, um, share?" (Like your father wanted, she added silently.)

"Well, I've always felt the island should be kept as a unit. It's been that way for what, a hundred and twenty-five years? One owner at a time. Dad often had opportunities to sell parcels to cottagers, quite profitably, but he always refused. He said he wanted Stone Face Island to remain a whole, the way an island should be. And I feel the same way."

"Understandable," Matt said lazily. "But it's my island too. Suppose I made you an offer?"

Noel laughed gently. "You couldn't afford it."

"But suppose I scraped up the money? I could. I have friends."

"I don't deal in suppositions."

Matt pushed back his chair with a clatter and walked to the balustrade. He turned around to face the row of faces. "I guess Sheila told you about the latest Jack incident?"

"Yes." Noel watched him carefully.

"He crashed my canoe, but that's nothing. He could have killed Cally. He put Ginny in danger too." He bit off each word. "I want him fired."

Sheila stood up. "Noel — I never thought I'd agree with Matt, but I do now. Jack's had enough chances."

Noel looked up at her unhappily. "I agree too, Sheila, but it's just that Dad hired him. You know how I feel about that."

"Even so. We can't let this go on."

"I'll talk to him. I promise."

"Talk!" Matt dug the flattened pack of cigarettes out of his shirt pocket and lit one. He waved the match out and tossed it into a flower bed below the terrace. A thread of smoke drifted up past the zinnias and into the glow of the citronella candle.

"Going to make sure of that match, Matthew?" Noel's tone was studiously friendly.

"Nothing there to burn. Still, just to set your mind at ease." Matt stepped down, poked his shoe among the zinnias, set his toe into the soft earth and ground it down. As he returned Noel gave him a bright, artificial smile. Cally's teeth went on edge.

"Well, Ginny!" Noel jumped from his chair, abruptly jolly. "Now let's have a game. What shall we play?"

"There's always Monopoly," Aubrey said. "Knowing Gin, she'd own the whole board within an hour."

"No, that's so boring," Gin objected cheerfully. The electric exchange between the brothers hadn't even touched her. "I know, let's play hide and seek! It's just dark enough to be spooky."

"Hide and seek!" Noel clapped his hands. "Perfect!"

Sheila frowned up at him. "Isn't that a bit too childish even for Gin?"

"What's wrong with being childish once in a while?" He laughed. "Don't you always tell me I don't unbend enough? Cally, are you in?" He held out his hands.

"Why not?" She could use a little childish nonsense herself right now. She stood up and stretched the tightness out of her shoulders.

"Let's go! Aubrey, you're It!" Noel grabbed her hand and pulled her down the terrace steps and across the lawn toward the woods.

Matt shouted something that she couldn't make out.

They stopped on the path at the edge of the woods. The young moon barely touched the darkness here. Cally pulled her hand free. "Aren't you supposed to be hiding?"

"We could hide together." He moved closer, his smile warm and teasing.

This was a very strange mood for Noel, who was always so correct. She'd never seen him like this. Perhaps he'd had too much wine? But that wouldn't be like him either.

Everyone seemed to be in a strange mood tonight. There was a wildness in the air, a sense that normality had been left behind, that they had strayed into unknown territory.

"We could curl up under the pines, just the two of us." His eyes gleamed.

"Oh, no! Two can't hide in one spot. Them's the rules!" She pushed him away. He laughed and melted into the leafy darkness. In a moment even the sound of him was gone. She was alone.

Chapter 12

HARDLY ABLE to see, Cally felt her way gingerly with her bare feet down the uneven slope from the path. After a few steps she knew it was a bad idea, walking around in the woods without shoes. The ground was thick with prickly things, pine cones and bits of twig and small stones. And probably squirrel scat and dew worms and who knew what all.

She stretched out her arms in front to fend off branches and the boles of trees, and discovered a big silver birch, its pale bark just visible in the dark. She slipped around to the far side and leaned her back against it. This made as good a hiding place as any.

Now that she had stopped moving, the night sounds of the forest rose around her. Trill and chirrup of insect, the rustle of dry stems in the small breeze, the silky whisper of green leaves. High above, a nighthawk's call. And under all these, weaving them together, the ceaseless whisper of wavelets on the beach. Cally let her head rest against the bark. So peaceful here, all alone.

Only she wasn't alone. She lifted her head. There it was again, a faint crackle in the duff of dry pine needles. She stared wide-eyed in that direction but nobody materialized out of the darkness.

Silence, then, for the space of a dozen heartbeats. Then a long rushy sound, something sliding through dry leaves. Something smooth and stealthy and snakelike. Cally inched her bare feet closer to the tree trunk. She remembered that there were massasauga rattlers in this region.

I don't like this. Not one bit.

An airy flutter on her cheek, and Cally cried out. Then mocked herself silently. Only a moth! *Scared of the dark, Cally?*

That sliding sound again. A cold touch on her ankle. Horror froze her to silence. Her heart thudded in her ears, drowning out everything else.

Then common sense came to her rescue. A snake won't bite if you don't startle it, or so she'd heard, and anyway it was gone now. And probably it wasn't even a rattler. How stupid to panic like that! She laughed aloud, defiantly, not caring that the sound would carry.

Something echoed her laughter from the denser shadows deeper in the woods. A low, breathy chuckle.

That's it, I'm fed up with this game. "Aubrey? I give up. I'm here."

No answer except for a brief rustling, this time from the opposite direction, toward the house. Then a crickle-crackle up the hill. And that chuckle again. It seemed to her now that it had some of the sibilant quality of the wind whistling through the windows of the cottage.

Now there were small sounds all around her. She could see them clearly in her mind's theatre: *shadowy little people with glinting eyes and sharp fingers, creeping upon me in the dark. Closing in.*

Cally broke and made a dash for the path. Hands caught and held her. She yelled, struggled, wrenched free, and staggered.

"What the hell?" he said.

"Matt!"

"Who else?"

"Why were you trying to scare me? That wasn't funny!"

"What's the matter with you?" He lifted a hand and she flinched back. "Cally," he said softly. It was a reproach and a plea, and something more. It lanced into her heart and it hurt.

"I'm — I'm okay now."

88

"What was scaring you?"

"Noises, that's all. Night and the woods and small critters and my galloping imagination. I feel like an idiot."

"Well, it was an idiotic idea to start with, this game. Running around the woods in the dark, people getting poked and scratched — Noel should know better. I came straight here when I heard you crashing around. This yellow dress of yours shows up in the dark like a candle. Cally, I...."

She could still only see him as a large, dense shadow among frailer shadows. His warm skin scent came to her along with the tang of bruised leaves. Then his arms slipped around her and gathered her gently to his chest.

This is a mistake. A mistake. I'm losing my mind. But it was an indescribably sweet madness.

His breath in her hair. "Cally, you should leave."

"Wh... what?"

"You heard what I said earlier. Something's wrong, something's happening, and I don't know what it is. I just know it's dangerous. I wish you'd never come here." He opened his arms and held her off, hands cupped on her shoulders.

"What are you afraid of?"

"If I knew, I wouldn't be so worried. I wish we could get Gin away. The island's no place for her this summer. But of course Noel won't do anything I suggest." He drew in a deep breath and let his hands drop. "I wonder, would Sheila listen to you? If you could convince her, get her to use her pull with Noel, that might do it."

"I think I agree with you about Gin — just a feeling, I'm not sure why. And I'd be glad to talk to Sheila, only what argument would I use?"

He drew another deep breath, bracing himself. "Cally, If I tell you—"

"You get away from her!"

The shout in her ear was shattering. For a moment she was dazed with shock. Then she felt emptiness and knew Matt had stepped away.

A hand grabbed her arm. "Cally, are you all right?"

"Yes, Noel! I'm perfectly safe and sound!" She yanked her arm free, desperately needing to get away from them both. She blundered uphill to the path with Noel on her heels. Matt climbed more slowly after them.

Starlight touched down here, where the trees drew back. Enough light to show faces and the expressions on them. Noel was white with fear or fury. "What right—" she began hotly.

Matt cut across. "Noel, act your age." He was brusque and amused. "You're not Cally's dad. She can take care of herself."

"I am going for a walk," Cally said distinctly.

"I'll go with you," Noel said.

"No! Don't either of you dare come!"

EVERY NERVE in her body was standing on end and shrieking. If only, she thought as she strode along the path, if only I could take a breath and blow away this poisoned atmosphere! I'd even settle for a good rattling thunderstorm. Anything for a change in the weather.

When she came in sight of the cottage she stopped short. Alone, she had no wish to go anywhere near that place. To the left of the path, here, the trees gave way to light brush. She picked her way carefully down the slope, holding onto stems and branches, thinking to find a way down to the shore.

She found and followed a rough path that slanted steeply down the slope, then levelled out and slanted up again. Then she felt cool stone under her bare soles, and the sky was open overhead. The lake murmured and glinted far below. She had worked her way onto the southwest face of the cliff.

The drop wasn't as intimidating, just here, as it would become closer to the giant's face. From bottom to top it would be a strenuous climb, but there were plenty of tough cedars and firm footholds and no long, smooth planes.

All the same, it was a stupidly risky thing to do, climbing in the dark. She found a place to stop, a boulder that stuck out five feet below the top of the cliff. If you looked up at this spot from below, this might be one outer tip of the brow ridge.

I won't go any farther. I'll sit here and enjoy the quiet and being alone. I'll think of nothing. Half an hour here and maybe I'll be able to sleep.

A voice suddenly spoke out over her head, startling her so that she nearly slipped off her boulder. Cally looked up, but nobody was standing there. After an uneasy moment she climbed up onto the boulder and peered over the brink of the cliff.

A figure sat on the ground not two yards distant. Out in the open, the sky glow was bright enough to show that it was a man, and he sat with his back turned to her. Beside him on the ground he held something that winked glassily. He was facing the cottage. Its recessed doorway was a gaping black mouth, Cally thought, and wished she hadn't.

"No, I haven't," he said grumpily. It was Jack Beamish. A pause, as if to hear a reply. Then he went on, "I tell you I'm doing all I can."

In the pause that followed, Cally strained eyes and ears to locate the other person. There was nobody. Jack's voice was pitched at a normal level. He seemed to be speaking to the cottage itself. Or to someone inside, standing at one of the cat's-eye windows. But the door was locked, so how could anyone get inside?

"Yeah, I know they got no right. Many's the time I told 'em so."

Silence.

"Yeah, right to their ugly faces!"

Silence.

"Well, no. They got papers, there's the trouble."

A longer silence, while Jack hunched his shoulders. His next re-mark sounded abject.

"I'm sorry, Great-granddad. I'll do better, I swear."

Cally stared in horror.

"Yeah ... yeah... we do have that." Sly and knowing now. "Piece of work, that girl, eh?" He sniggered. "Guess she got what was comin' to her. Yeah, I been usin' that, some."

Silence.

"You're right, there's deep pockets there. But I got to be careful, eh? Can't push. Could be risky. You never know with that one." Then he listened. "Granddad?" Listened again. Then snorted. "Dead drunk again, the old sod."

He manoeuvred himself with difficulty to a standing position. Cally ducked down. When she lifted her head again, he was bending to pick up the gleaming thing: a bottle. He staggered, caught his bal-ance, upended the bottle into his mouth, then clutched it to his chest and tottered away past the cottage. In a moment he was lost in the darkness under the trees. Cally was left alone, with the cottage squat-ting much too near and hints of madness plucking at her overstrained nerves.

Poor Jack! The bee in his bonnet about the ownership of the cot-tage had finally buzzed right through his brain. He seemed to think he had some weapon — some piece of information? — that he'd already been using in some way.

But what was it? Who was this "girl" who had "got what was coming to her"? And who was Jack's target? Whoever it was, he was wary of him or her.

Cally shook her head. Most likely it was nothing but moonshine. If Jack could sit and chat with a ghost, he might imagine anything.

She scrambled back across the cliff until the slope gentled. Here she climbed to the top, found the stone dust path, and followed it back. She had been out for perhaps half an hour. The time out hadn't been calming, but she was tired. Maybe tired enough to sleep.

Midway between the cottage and the house, the path passed through the densest stretch of woods. No light penetrated the canopy of leaves. She walked slowly here, only the hard smoothness of the path guiding her feet.

Behind her, on the path, came a soft footfall. Cally whirled around, her heart thudding. "Who's there?"

No answer. She backed away. Nothing came after her. She stood still and tried to search the darkness. Nothing moved.

Imagination. That's all it was.

She turned and started off again. A broken glow lay ahead where the trees drew back again from the path and the house lights showed through. She walked faster, aiming for that glow. Her heart still thumped ridiculously.

It came in a rush from behind, a flurry of running footsteps, a hard push, and gone. Cally pitched off the path. Something cracked against her forehead. The air before her eyes broke up into sparkling motes and she was falling.

Chapter 13

"CALLY! What happened?"

With Sheila's help, Cally sat up. Then stood up, bracing herself with a hand against a tree, probably the same one that had knocked her silly. "I fell off the path and hit my head."

"Oh no! How bad?"

"Not concussion, I don't think. I'll live."

"You should know you can't go walking in the dark, it's not safe!"

"It's perfectly safe." Cally shuffled back to the path. "Or would be, if people didn't run up from behind and knock me down!"

"What?"

They started slowly back down the path toward the house, arm in arm. Cally described what happened in a few words. "And the next thing I knew, you were there. What brought you out?"

"Noel told me you'd run off to get away from Matt—"

"And from Noel—"

"And then I thought you'd been gone a long time and I went looking."

Cally stopped and gripped her wrist. "Did you see anybody as you came along the path?"

"Not a soul."

"Huh. Where was everybody?"

"Counting suspects, are we?" Sheila sounded grimly amused. They started down the path again. "I'd say the field's wide open. I'm guessing nobody has an alibi for ... what, ten minutes ago?"

"Maybe that."

"The hide and seek fell apart as soon as Aubrey found me, which wasn't hard because I wasn't really hiding. Then Noel came back in. He's in the parlour now, reading *Report on Business*. Aubrey found Gin in the back pantry, hiding in a lower cupboard with the potatoes. Obviously Matt helped her get in there. He was in the kitchen brewing coffee when I left. Mrs. Gardner and Edna...."

"We'll count them out. And it wasn't Gin, and I'll take it on faith that it wasn't you."

"Gee, thanks!"

"Which leaves who?"

"First off, what about Jack? I've no idea where he's been or where he is now."

"Jack's out of it." She told how she'd ended up on the cliff face, which made Sheila's breath hiss in. "I saw Jack up there near the cottage, mumbling away." She hesitated, then decided to keep that one-sided dialogue to herself for a while. It needed thinking about. "He left before I did. Anyway, it couldn't be him. He could barely stagger, let alone run."

The path led them out of the woods and onto the lawn. Cally stopped there and gazed across at the house. Lights were on all over. It looked warm and welcoming, a great golden ship on a dark sea. Yet it bristled with secrets.

"It wasn't Noel, anyway. He'd never be such a jerk," Sheila said decidedly. "If he ever accidentally knocked you over he'd stop and pick you up, all apologies. And I don't think it was Aubrey, either."

"Any special reason?" Cally smiled.

"No. I just don't." Sheila sounded cross, which meant she was ruffled.

"Aha!"

"Aha nothing." Sheila started across the lawn, pulling Cally with her. "Wait, what about smell? Did you smell anything? Like, tobacco smoke? A smoker would stink of it."

"I know who you mean, and no. Besides, I don't think it could be him, either."

"Aha, eh? So who's left?"

"Nobody. It had to be an outsider." Relief broke over her like light. "That's it! It must have been one of those boys from the village. He ran into me on the path, got scared he'd be in trouble, and panicked. That's got to be it."

"Hm, don't like the sound of that — strangers running amok on the island."

"Isn't it better than thinking it's one of us?"

"Right. I suppose we'd better tell the police."

They found everyone in the parlour, including Matt, who was leaning in the doorway nursing a mug of coffee and listening to Ginevra play the piano. When Sheila tersely described Cally's encounter Noel went white with alarm, then spluttered with indignation. Matt brushed him aside and searched Cally's eyes for signs of concussion.

"Unresponsive pupils are bad," he explained, cupping her face in one hand and shining a pocket flashlight into her eyes with the other. "Yours work fine. And you appear to have all your wits." He gazed a moment longer than he needed to before switching off the flashlight. Cally blinked away purple blotches.

When Sheila raised the question of reporting the incident to the police, Matt volunteered for the job. "You'll have to come with me, though." He pointed the flashlight sternly at Cally.

"I should go, Matt," Noel said evenly. "Cally is here because I engaged her, remember?"

"Yes, but this thing happened on my part of the island. I'll go." Matt turned away and went upstairs.

"THEY WERE a fat lot of help, weren't they?"

Matt let the glass door slam behind them. The Ontario Provincial Police detachment office in Port Devon, twenty miles south of Blackwater Bay, was a modest red-brick building near the marina. Apart from the sign and the OPP crest, it was identical to the tackle shop across the street.

"They were awfully pleasant and polite about it, though," Cally said. "Considering there was really nothing they could do but take my statement. Promising to run a patrol boat around the island once a day was probably more than we could've hoped for, don't you think? We could hardly expect an on-site armed guard."

The three regular and two marine officers of the Port Devon detachment had more than enough to do coping with overenthusiastic hunters, aggressive boaters and drunk drivers, Matt and Cally had been told. They hadn't the manpower to investigate every case of trespassing among the thirty-some islands that dotted Lake St. Jude's twisting length. The promise of a regular patrol was a generous concession.

"I'll bet it was just some kid, and he was as scared as me. We won't see any more of him." She was determined to put the incident behind her, but knew she was trying too hard. Matt gave her a smiling look that said she wasn't fooling him.

"Long as we're here," he said, "let's be tourists." He stuck his hands in his jeans pockets and started strolling.

They both badly needed a change of scene. Cally had been looking forward all morning to the trip. They wandered among the stalls of the farmers' market, stopping whenever she spotted something

97

fascinating, which was often. They bought slabs of soft gingerbread and washed it down with cups of cloudy cider. They watched the boats flocking in and out of the marina like exotic birds, all in vibrant reds and blues and yellows, and sparkling whites.

It felt like a holiday. Stone Face Island and its poisoned atmosphere might have been half the world away. Matt relaxed as she'd never seen him do before. And every other minute they discovered something new about each other. That they both loved old movies and buttered popcorn, and Toronto in September but not in January. That Cally couldn't pass any kind of second-hand store without going in, while Matt was addicted to hardware stores. That both loved their work.

"You're good for me." He stopped abruptly on the boardwalk and looked down at her, not caring who bumped into them. "You get so much joy out of life. And it's catching."

This, Cally thought, would be the right moment to tackle him about some of the questions Noel and Sheila had raised in her mind. Then she shook the thought away. These few hours together had been perfect — *and damned if I'll spoil them.*

As they walked back through the thick afternoon sunshine toward the slip where they'd berthed the motorboat, a startling happiness cascaded through her mind and body. She quickly rapped the nearest wooden object, a handrail along the boardwalk.

"Touching wood, Cally? I didn't know you were superstitious."

"I'm not. Or I didn't used to be. Just now I can't help thinking it's unlucky to feel so good."

He laughed, then reached out and tapped the rail beside her.

KNOCK WOOD. The thought came back to her as she stood outside Sheila's bedroom door. Her knuckles hovered an inch from the panel.

Then she changed her mind. Instead of knocking, she pushed the door open and went in.

Sheila occupied two adjoining rooms at the southwest corner of the second floor. The bedroom was cluttered and messy. By contrast the studio, beyond, was kept in regimented order. It was furnished with worktable, drafting table, shelves, cupboards and a sink. No rugs, no drapes, nothing unnecessary.

The setting sun flooded the room with gold and haloed Sheila's dark hair. She glanced up briefly as Cally came in, then returned her attention to the sketch pad propped on her knee. Her hand never stopped its quick movement across the page. It was a coloured pastel drawing of Ginevra, the face almost finished, the rest still rough.

Cally stood watching quietly, knowing not to interrupt while Sheila was at work. It was almost worth the wait. The picture deserved a good long look, even in its unfinished state. It showed Ginny perched on a rock in the garden. Nothing suggested her disability. She looked whole and eager, ready to lift off like a bird. At the same time the soft vivid masses of flowers that framed the slight, poised figure were like a yielding but protective shield.

There was love in that picture. All the love, Cally thought, that Sheila couldn't express, and Ginny couldn't even guess at.

She stood quietly for five minutes. Then ten. Then she lost patience. "Are we going to talk about it?"

"About what?" Sheila went on sketching.

"About that look you gave me when Matt and I got back from Port Devon. Just about sliced my head off! And after that — nothing. As if I'd stopped existing."

Sheila's hand moved faster, more raggedly. Finally the chalk snapped and she threw the stubs on the floor. She stared at the sketch, her mouth tight.

99

"All right." Cally turned and headed for the door.

"Cal."

She stopped, took a calming breath, in and out, and turned again.

"I'm not angry," Sheila said. "I'm afraid. Afraid for you."

"Because I spent the afternoon with Matt, and enjoyed it? But he isn't what you think he is. I don't know why you—"

"I knew this would happen." Sheila stood up and slapped the sketch book onto a table. "You've let him hoax you. You're not thinking, you're just seeing him the way he wants you to."

"And you see him how? Like this?" Cally waved at the walls around them, where completed sketches were taped. Among them were smaller versions of the pictures she'd seen in the university gallery. "What does all this really mean? How can I take it seriously? I mean, look at this!"

She marched to the wall and glared at a study of Matt standing over the prone body of a woman: a version of the one he'd paid a thousand dollars for. As in the other pictures, the male figure was brutally triumphant, the female figure destroyed and desolate.

"Who is she, anyway?"

"Who?"

"This woman in the pictures with Matt. Who is she?"

Sheila shrugged and walked to the window. "Nobody in particular. She's a symbol."

"Don't give me that. You made Matt's figure so particular, so real. How can you tell me this scene isn't based on anything real?"

"Leave it, Cally."

"I can't. It means too much to me."

"Me too." Sheila turned. The sun was behind her, hiding her expression. "Cal, I think it may be best if you don't stay here any longer."

"What's that mean?"

"I mean you should leave. Today, if possible. Before something happens."

It was hard to talk past the sudden lump in her throat. "That sounds like a threat. What happened to my best friend?"

"It's not a threat. Don't you understand, Cal? I'm doing my best to protect you!"

"Because of that mugger yesterday? Or, no, it's because I've been asking questions, isn't it? What is this terrible thing about Matt you can't tell me? Who is that woman in the pictures?"

"Look, Cally, if you can't have a little faith—"

"If you can't be honest with me—"

"Cally, I'm telling you for your own good! Just go away!" Sheila's mouth was set hard and Cally knew that she, too, was fighting tears.

Chapter 14

CALLY RAN DOWN the stairs, out the open front door and across the lawn. She flew toward the cottage like a bee straight for the hive. Halfway along the forest path she slowed down to think what she was doing.

By the time she came out onto the meadow, where the dry turf glowed yellow in the evening sunshine, she knew what her choices were.

After the heat outside, it was cool and dark in the cottage. Matt didn't see her at once. His back was turned to the doorway and the roar of a portable generator covered the sound of her footsteps. He was using an electric sander to smooth a plank clamped in a vise. She walked around to where he could see her, and he switched off the generator.

"I'm making new shutters." He smiled at her, with all the afternoon's happiness in his eyes. "Using the old ones as a pattern."

She ran her hand over the piece of wood, where he'd sanded it. "Feels lovely. Satiny. And it smells so good!"

He rubbed his hand across the plank after hers. Somehow their hands collided and enfolded each other. The incense of pine dust rose around them.

He was too near, her awareness of him too intense. She slipped her hand from his and took a step back. The distance was necessary for what she had to say.

"Tell me about Vanessa."

The light faded from his face. He shook his head slightly, turned away and reached for the generator's on/off switch. Its din rose like a wall between them. Cally struggled with herself, then turned and made for the door.

On the threshold he caught her and swung her around to face him. "Where d'you think you're going?" He yelled it over the noise of the machine.

"Back to the house to pack!" She wrenched free and stepped out onto the turf.

"Now wait just a — Hold on!" He ducked back into the cottage and a moment later silence fell. Then he was back with thunder on his forehead. "Why?"

"I tried to get things straight with Sheila just now. No good. She said I should leave the island. You've said that too. And now you're shutting me out again. Why should I stay?"

"Some things...." His eyes left her face and scanned the horizon. "Just let it lie, Cally."

"That's what Sheila said. Leave it alone! But I can't live that way, Matt. There's all this — this witch's brew — simmering under the surface of things. Pretty soon it's going to boil over, and people are going to get hurt."

"And you figure your job is to dial down the heat?" He smiled one-sidedly. "It's not your problem, Cally."

"Isn't it?" She challenged him with a look.

"Why should it be?"

"Because Sheila's my friend. And I care about you."

"When you say 'you', you mean...." He cleared his throat. "Singular or plural?"

She took a breath. "I mean you, Matt."

"Oh God." He studied his hands. "No. It's not safe. You have to go." He looked up, a light kindling in his face. "When I get back to

Toronto, we—"

"Not good enough." She watched his brows draw together again. "No, Matt, this isn't a case of emotional blackmail. I'm not playing games. I'm just telling you how it is. I can't live with lies and secrets."

He hesitated a moment too long. Something like a block of ice formed and thickened under her breastbone. Her eyes fell and she turned and walked away.

A thud of sneakers on the turf. He caught her wrist again and pulled her to a stop. "You win. Come back inside, so I can work. I need to have my hands busy while I talk."

THEY SAT CROSS-LEGGED among the sawdust and wood shavings. Matt had begun rubbing an emery block across the cut end of the short pine plank, but now his hand grew still.

"Vanessa," he said. "You know, she was actually much more attractive than Sheila's portrait of her, because the picture doesn't even hint at the aliveness of her. She had so much energy you could've lit light bulbs off her. She wanted everything out of life, and then some. Loved the riskier sports, loved speed, got a kick out of a good loud fight. Yeah, we fought a lot." He showed his teeth, not exactly smiling.

"We were together for almost a year, and it was like having a fireworks show on day and night. Always exhilarating, but after a while a bit wearing. But I didn't get a chance to find out how long I could stand it, because one day we went to a party and Noel was there. Later I found out he'd been meeting Vanessa other places — 'accidentally' — and dropping hints that she'd improve her lot in life by making a change. I didn't know that then, but when he made eye contact at that party something told me he had an agenda. That put me at my worst, and I guess you know the rest."

"Are you saying he set out deliberately to steal your girlfriend?"

He let out a brief laugh and went back to smoothing the plank. "And succeeded. Sounds pathetic, doesn't it? But yes."

"Why, just to be obnoxious?"

"Mostly to score points, I think. He's always imagined there was some competition going on between us."

"Was there?"

"Not then, not now. At least not on my side. Pain in the ass, that's all it is. Anyway, that's when the fireworks went out. I never wanted to see Vanessa again."

"But you did," she said carefully.

"I did. That summer I came to the island and there she was. Noel had brought her to meet the whole family, charm Dad and so on. He said they were engaged. And then damned if she didn't start sending signals!" He shook his head, incredulous. "A touch here, a word there. I finally got what she meant. She wanted us to pick up where we'd left off, the winter before.

"Even then I mistook her." His mouth crooked down, mocking himself. "I thought she meant she was tired of Noel and still wanted me and we should go away together. For me that was a non-starter, after the way she'd sloughed me off."

"Wait, you mean she didn't love Noel?"

"Love! Well, she loved the idea of marrying Noel. She loved the security, financial and otherwise. She suggested we carry on discreetly under his nose. Dear sweet, naive Noel need never know a thing about it."

He caught her eyes and grinned. "Yeah. I have a strong stomach, but that turned it. I arranged to meet her up here at the cottage one evening so I could spell it out for her. I told her exactly what I thought of her. She threw a tantrum. I went back to the house and she stayed behind at the cottage, too mad to show her face." He added, "I don't know if anybody saw her after that. Next morning she was gone."

"Did you ever tell this to Noel or Sheila?"

"I tried to tell Sheila once. She wouldn't let me finish. I could never find out why she loathes me."

Loathes? Cally started to protest, then closed her mouth. He was right, it was that extreme.

She looked around the cottage. "Why does it always feel so cold in here?" She rubbed at the goose bumps on her upper arms. "Can we get out of here, please?"

They picked up and moved to a grassy spot near the edge of the cliff. The sun perched on the horizon like a big red Chinese lantern. Cool air from across the lake tangled with heat rising from the rocks and blew Cally's hair across her eyes. She pushed it back.

"What do you think really happened to Vanessa?"

Matt nursed a bottle of beer he'd brought from a cooler in the cottage. Drops of condensation ran down his arm. After a long silence he sighed, shook his head, tilted the bottle and drank.

"I can't get those pictures of Sheila's out of my mind," she persisted. "You know the ones I mean?"

"I paid a thousand bucks for one of them, thanks to you, remember?" His voice was very dry. "You're looking at the star of Sheila's darkest fantasy, Cally."

"But is it a fantasy?"

The bottle thumped on the turf. "You mean you believe—"

"What those pictures seem to say?" She laughed scornfully. "If I did, would I be here with you?"

He captured her hand and gave it a squeeze. Then let it go. "I wish I could tell you where Sheila got that image, but I can't."

Cally picked at the grass beside her as she worried at the idea. "How did she and Vanessa get along? Did they quarrel?"

"Not outright. Sheila just turned a cold shoulder. Vanessa thought that was funny."

"Sheila thinks you scared her off."

"Huh! Vanessa didn't scare that easy."

"She did leave awfully suddenly."

"Well, if somebody scared her off, it wasn't me. I didn't care enough."

Cally thought of Jack's cryptic conversation with his ghostly great-great-granddad. Could he have been talking about Sheila? Or Noel? But what could Jack possibly know that would hurt either of them?

"You're wondering if she was murdered."

She looked up, startled, and he nodded at her. "The way you're hugging yourself, it isn't hard to guess. But you can forget that, Cally. She packed her things and went away and that's all there is to it. She doesn't matter now."

But even as they walked, hand in hand like sweethearts, down the forest path toward the house, Cally knew she hadn't convinced herself. And she suspected Matt hadn't convinced himself either. Something of Vanessa still troubled the island, like a ghost whose only manifestation was a trace of perfume on the evening air.

Chapter 15

SOMETHING FUNDAMENTAL had changed between Cally and Matthew. He behaved like a man who had been sick for a long time, so long that he'd forgotten what it was like to feel really well. And now that illness was behind him. He seemed full of energy, optimism and appetite, delighting Mrs. Gardner with his appreciation of her cooking.

After dinner he, Cally and Ginevra spent a long, lazy evening on the terrace. Their conversation ranged over every subject under the sun. Cally hadn't laughed so much since she couldn't remember when.

The other three faded as night fell. Cally noticed that they had fallen, the six of them, into a new pattern. Before, it was the twins sitting side-by-side in chairs on the terrace and Aubrey moving restlessly between them and Cally and Ginevra. Now it was Cally, Matt and Ginevra all in a row, then a space, and then Aubrey and Sheila elbow-to-elbow, with Noel behind and a little to the side, a minor outer planet. Aubrey murmured things that made Sheila laugh and glow.

Sheila said nothing to anyone else except once, when she paused by Matt's chair before going inside and said, "I would like to take your canoe out tomorrow morning, please. Is that all right?"

Matt blinked up at her. "Of course it's all right!"

"And I would like to take Aubrey with me. Is that all right?"

"Of course! Sheila, for God's sake, you don't have to—"

"Thank you," she said, and walked away. Matt looked after her with a bleak look in his eyes. Cally longed to take his hand; but no, not in public like this.

Noel said nothing but he watched everybody. Especially, he watched Matthew.

WEDNESDAY morning, Cally stood in the open front doorway and looked out over the flower beds and lawn. In the shadows the grass glittered with dew. Beyond that the world was softened: trees, water, faraway shoreline all melted into a silver haze.

"Up already?" said a voice from up the stairs.

She turned, looked up and beamed as Sheila came down. "I woke up and heard the birds and went out to join them," Cally said. "I've already had breakfast."

"Well, make the most of the moment. It's going to be hot as hell later on." Sheila had braided her hair into a single plait for coolness and put on shorts and a halter top. She carried a wide-brimmed, flower-trimmed straw hat in one hand and looked bright-eyed and pretty.

"Something's doing you good." Cally looked her over. "What is it, the fresh air and sunshine, or Aubrey?"

"Or both?" Sheila's smile touched her eyes.

Cally tweaked at her own T-shirt and jeans. "Look at me. You're already dressed for the heat."

"Dressed for canoeing. Aubrey and I are going out on the lake. Early, while the sun's low."

Aubrey came clattering down, glowing in white shorts and T-shirt. He danced along the hall to catch Sheila by the waist and whirl her around. She pushed him away, laughing; then caught Cally's eye, flushed, and stepped out onto the terrace.

Cally grabbed Aubrey before he could follow. "Hey, you. Wait.

109

You'll be careful, right?"

"Me careful? Sheila's the expert boater and swimmer. I'm counting on her to save me if we sink."

"I don't mean the canoeing. I mean you and her." She moved closer and lowered her voice. "If you hurt her I swear I'll eviscerate you."

"Don't get yourself in a twist." His voice lilted, but his eyes held nothing lightsome. "More likely to be the other way round."

"You're kidding."

"Nope."

"Aubrey! Are we going?" Sheila called from the terrace. He gave Cally a wave and ran out the door.

THE MORNING'S lesson started on the terrace, on the shady west side. By ten-thirty the tide of sunshine had rolled across the lawn to their feet. When Edna appeared with a tray of iced fruit juices, Cally put down her book with a sigh of relief.

Ginevra shut hers with a final-sounding slap. "We should be reading a translation. They translate Chaucer, why not Shakespeare?"

"Because Shakespeare wrote in modern English," Cally said, biting back a laugh.

"So you say." Ginny glugged juice. "This is silly, reading this useless junk. I'd learn lots more up at the cottage helping Matt."

"Like what?"

"Oh ... measuring. Carpentry. You know." She waved an airy hand. "Proper use of tools. I'm going straight up there soon as this lesson's over, and no, I won't need any help."

Hm. How to put this without being too interfering? "You know, Matt's really fussy about that cottage. He doesn't exactly welcome visitors when he's working, so—"

"Oh, but I'm welcome! He said so. Lots of times." Ginny radiated happiness like a miniature sun. Then she gave Cally an oddly adult, appraising look from under wrinkled eyebrows. "He said you're welcome too. He said so last night. He said I should tell you. So I have."

"Oh. Good." Cally picked up her glass and took a drink.

"Um. Cally." There was a new, careful note in Ginny's voice. "Are you, um...."

"Yes? Am I what?"

"Are you going to marry him?"

Cally choked. When she finished coughing she cleared her throat, shook her head, and laughed.

Ginevra folded her arms across her chest. "It's not a joke. I can tell he likes you a lot. And you like him, right?"

"Yes, but that doesn't always mean–"

"Well, I kind of like you too, so I won't mind if you marry him. But just remember, you've got to take me in. If I have to have a guardian, I want it to be Matt, not Noel."

Cally set down her glass and picked up her book. "We're getting really off-topic. Where were we?"

"No idea." Ginny pushed away her book with the back of her hand. "Matt should've been my guardian in the first place. He's the oldest, so it would only be right. Besides, he's special to me and Noel doesn't even like me."

"Gin, I'm sure that's not true. Besides, your father made that decision. He must have had his reasons. And now...." She picked up Ginny's book, opened it and pushed it across the table. "Let's get on with our review!"

Ginevra contorted her lovely face into a grimace of disgust. She dragged the book onto her lap as if it were a ten-pound world atlas instead of a lightweight paperback. Then a voice called from the beach.

"Visitors!" Gin chirped, and pushed the book off her knees. She buzzed away at top speed to the ramp and the lawn, and the path that led down to the pier.

Cally groaned and pushed sweat-sodden tendrils off her forehead. "Anything to avoid work!" She got up and headed for the path. Gin had halted her wheelchair halfway down and now turned, her face bright and excited.

"It's not visitors, it's Sheila! And no canoe! Something's happened to Aubrey!"

"THE CANOE SANK," Sheila said. "About two miles southwest of here. We swam to a small island, really just a rock, and tried to get the attention of passing boaters. But wouldn't you know it, for once none of them came near. So I swam back."

Sheila sat on the pier, swinging and flexing her legs, and looking both weary and furious.

"Two miles! And Aubrey?" Noel said anxiously. He had been working in the library, something to do with business, and he'd come at a run when Cally called him.

Sheila shook her head. "He can't swim that far or anything like it. So he's marooned on a rock the size of a suitcase."

"And Jack's taken the inboard to Port Devon," Noel said.

"We'll go rescue him!" Ginevra whirled her wheelchair enthusiastically. "I'll get Matt and he can drive the little white boat."

"Not Matt," Noel said heavily. "I'll go. Sheila, you come along and show me where."

They returned twenty minutes later, with Aubrey looking sunburned and wilted, and more than a little ridiculous in Sheila's

112

flower-trimmed straw hat. She had lent it to him as a sunshield while he waited on the rock. Cally wasn't able to stifle a laugh, but he didn't take offense. After climbing onto the pier, he swept off the hat in an extravagant bow, then offered it to Sheila with a flourish.

She took it and tied it on, smiling. "Nothing ever hurts your dignity, does it? I like that."

"He doesn't have any dignity to *get* hurt," Cally said.

Noel tied up the boat and they started up the path to the house. "So, how did it happen?" Cally asked. "Did you capsize?"

"No," Sheila said. "A capsized canoe will float. Ought to. Something else happened."

"Well?"

"I'm going to take it up with Matt." There was a grim note in her voice.

Noel touched her hand. "D'you really think that's wise?" She shrugged.

Cally was about to burst out with questions when Mrs. Gardner appeared at the top of the path. "Is Ginevra with you? She's not anywhere in the house. Edna's putting lunch on the table and I can't spare her to go chasing all over the island after that child."

"She said she meant to go up to the cottage," Cally said. "I'll go see."

"We'll all go," Sheila said firmly. "Aubrey, you too."

Noel lifted his hands, palms outward. "If you'll excuse me, I'd like to get a little more work done before lunch." He turned toward the house. Cally guessed he knew there was a confrontation brewing and he was backing off.

They made a silent procession across the lawn and up the path under the trees. Sheila walked in front, then Aubrey, then Cally. It was too hot to waste energy on speed or conversation. A shiver ran

113

up Cally's spine and she wasn't sure if it was apprehension or anticipation.

They emerged from the humid shade of the woods into the meadow at the tip of the island. The grass was like straw, reflecting the sun yellowly and sending up shimmering heat waves. They plodded around the corner of the cottage and stopped in an awkward cluster. Sheila's breath hissed in and she sank her nails into Cally's wrist.

Matt stood on the brink of the cliff, feet apart, hands at his sides. His back was turned and he gazed out over the hazy blue reaches of the lake. It made Cally think of Sheila's portrait of him, the one that had troubled her dreams.

There were differences. The storm clouds and the ace of spades were missing. In the picture, also, Matt had been alone on the cliff. Here, he stood beside Ginevra's wheelchair. But the chair was empty.

Chapter 16

ANOTHER MOMENT and Cally guessed the answer. "Wait!" she said. "It's not what—"

But Sheila was already sprinting across the meadow, Aubrey at her heels. Matt turned as they came. He looked first surprised, then guarded. Sheila planted herself in front of him.

"Where's Gin?" It was an accusation.

He stared into her face, then glanced at the empty wheelchair. Then back at her. Red crested his cheekbones.

"Answer me! Where is she?"

He looked past her at Cally, an urgent question in his eyes. She shook her head and tried to smile.

"Is it lunchtime?" A voice piped up from behind him, and below. Ginevra's face appeared at foot level, laughing up at them.

Sheila shook with the shock of relief. "What are you doing down there?"

"I'm sitting. There's a rock here just right for sitting and looking."

Stepping closer, Cally saw that Ginny was perched on a rock a little above the boulder where she herself had sat two nights ago, listening to Jack Beamish converse with a ghost. She'd guessed it had to be something like that.

"How did you get down?" she asked.

"Matt lifted me down, of course." She giggled. "Whatcha think, I climbed?"

"Well," Sheila said. "That's not a safe spot. And yes, it is lunchtime. So, Matt, if you'd be so kind?"

Matt knelt and reached down, took hold of Ginny under the arms, lifted her and stood up. Cally moved the wheelchair into position and held it while Matt set her down. Gin swung the chair around and started off, then swung back. "You guys coming?"

"Wait." Sheila spoke directly to Matt. "I don't like Ginny being up here so much. It's not safe and it's not healthy."

Matt held her eyes a moment, then looked away. He hadn't yet spoken. Cally watched him uneasily. He was like a boiler under pressure.

"That's silly!" Ginevra scowled up at Sheila. "I can come here any time I like, Matt says so!"

"Matt is not your guardian."

"But it's not fair! I want—"

"Time for you to leave, Ginevra."

"No! I won't!"

"Aubrey, take Gin back now, please."

"You coming?" He caught her eye. She shook her head.

"I have something else to say."

"I'd rather stay with you."

"Cally will stay. You go."

They exchanged glances again. Aubrey frowned and began to push the chair over the tussocky ground toward the path, with Gin objecting loudly all the way.

Matt waited, still silent. Sheila faced him, white under her tan, hands hooked in the pockets of her still-damp shorts to still their trembling. "You and your canoe," she said evenly. "Aubrey might have drowned. Did you think of that?"

He squinted at her. "What?"

"The canoe sank," Cally said.

"Damn! How?"

"The crack," Sheila said. "The one you patched the other day? It opened again. The canoe filled with water and down it went."

Cally asked: "Did you crash? There could be submerged rocks near the surface."

"There wasn't so much as a bump." Sheila's eyes still stabbed at Matt's face. "Just a slight brush."

"That should have done no harm," he said.

"It wouldn't have if you'd done the job right."

"I did the job right," he said, quiet and slow. "I've fixed that kind of damage before."

"I know. You're usually so competent."

The air between them was all but smoking. Cally jumped in, hoping to cool things down: "It still shouldn't have sunk. What about those float bags that go in the ends?"

"I was wondering about them myself," Sheila said. "When I looked at the canoe last night they were in place. This morning I didn't check." Cally could have kicked herself. She'd made things worse.

Matt shook his head hard. "What are you saying? That I did it on purpose? Trashed a perfectly good canoe just to be nasty? Sheila, for the love of God!"

Sheila backed away a half step. Cally said, "Of course she doesn't mean that! That would be incredibly irresponsible! Anybody could have taken it out — it could have been me, or somebody could have taken Gin out."

"No, Cally. He knew it would be me. I asked him last night, re-member?"

"But why?" Cally waved her arms. "What for? He knows you're a strong swimmer — you're the best among us. So—"

"True. But if I were caught in the centre of the lake far from any land, even I might have drowned."

Matt leaned toward her and asked quietly, as if he really wanted to know: "What kind of a monster do you think I am?"

"Take your pick," Sheila said, just as quietly.

He stood for a moment shaking his head hard, like a bear attacked by bees. Then without another word he stalked around them and into the cottage. The door crashed shut behind him.

Cally gazed at Sheila. "You can't believe this."

"To tell the truth, I'm not sure what I believe." Sheila tramped back across the meadow toward the woods. "One thing I know, that canoe didn't sink by accident. And Matt didn't make any mistakes with the repair. He's good at things like that."

"Well, okay, then what about Jack Beamish? We know he resents Matt, because of the cottage, which he thinks is his." Cally waved backwards. "I bet he's mad because Matt put a lock on the door."

"Jack?" Sheila smiled thinly. "He's the one person who couldn't have done it. Did you notice he hasn't been around? He's been off the island since yesterday afternoon. Noel sent him to Port Devon to get spare parts for the generator. He may still be gone."

AFTER LUNCH, which only Ginevra and Aubrey seemed to enjoy, Cally carried a blanket to the shady side of the house and spread it out on the grass under the parasol of the encircling trees. There was no breeze, nothing to freshen the air indoors. She stretched out on her back, closed her eyes and listened to the distant tinkle of the piano — Ginevra tirelessly practicing — and thought of Matthew.

He hadn't asked her to stay, and that slam of the cottage door had a final sound. She wasn't about to trek up there just to get snubbed. All the signs said that Matt was the kind of man who didn't easily

118

share his feelings. Steady as a rock — so unlike Aubrey! — and as emotionally generous as a clam.

Oh, he had feelings, no doubt about that. They rayed out all over him like light from a leaky lampshade. And more and more she was sure that most of it was pain and sorrow. Yes, they'd had that golden afternoon together in Port Devon yesterday, they'd shared warmth and laughter. But that was then. And yes, he let his affection for Ginny show. But that was Ginny.

Cally laid a forearm over her eyes. If only Sheila would open up and explain what she had against the man! But Sheila was a clam too, when it came to feelings. What a family!

A change in the air and a deepening of shade roused her from a near-doze. She opened her eyes and looked up from under her arm at Noel, who was bent over gazing down at her. He drew back and pointed. "There's a caterpillar on your stomach."

Cally sat up with a squeak and picked the thing off and flung it away. She hated squirmy creatures. "Yuck! Thanks for the rescue." She squinted up at Noel, who was holding out a bottle of spring water. "And thanks again."

"Can you spare me a corner of your blanket?"

"Sure." She moved over and he lowered himself carefully, making sure no part of his spotless chinos touched the grass. He sat with his arms crossed over his bent knees, gazing down the hill through the trees toward the boathouse and the glinting lake. She studied him critically. He looked especially handsome just now, with his clean profile and the eyes that shone bluer than the lake in this bright light. A small breeze fingered back the fine ash-blond hair at his temples.

But with Noel, she reflected, what you saw was never exactly what you got. There was always something else. Something beneath.

"You look sad," she said, without intending to. But that was part of the trouble, she saw. That was what lay beneath his usually calm, quiet, smiling surface: a bone-deep, lifelong sadness. The shadow of something lost and forever missed.

He turned his head and smiled at her and the shadow went away. Now he looked focused and intent. "Sheila told me about that scene up at the cottage. I suppose you've been wondering about it. About what drives her, I mean."

"Among other things, yes, I was wondering about that."

"And of course you saw her pictures at the university show. Remember the one—"

"With the ace of spades? You bet. A stunner. And yes, I know what Sheila saw when we came out near the cliff today. I saw it too."

"Ah." He let go of his knees and stretched out his legs, then uncomfortably folded them back in again. "Should've brought a chair." He forced a smile. "There's a story behind that picture. I thought you should know it. All those pictures — most people think they're metaphors. Did you see the online review? All about Sheila's powerful deconstruction of male and female archetypes, and death and creation, and all that nonsense."

"I found the images confusing. They looked so much like Matt."

"That's because they *were* Matt."

"Um. Okay, and...."

"For years now she's been working through her feelings about him. She used her art to get through all that. She says it saved her life, or at least her sanity." He flashed a sapphire glance at her. "Her art, and you, Cally." He reached for her hand and gave it a brief squeeze, then let it go.

"I sorta knew all this, Noel. There's something else, isn't there?"

"Yes." He grimaced. "Right, better just plunge in. That ace of spades picture is an accurate record of what we saw, Sheila and I, the day of Francesca's death. Without the ace of spades, of course."

"What you saw?" Something sick and sour began to pool in Cally's stomach.

"What we saw, to be exact, a moment after she fell from the cliff." He paused to let that sink in. Then plowed on. "It was like this. Matt and Francesca were up at the island tip together, as they so often were. There was a storm building up — that's in the picture too — and Dad was worried. He wasn't well — his heart was starting to give him trouble — and he tended to get anxious. He worried about lightning strikes, for example. So he told Sheila to go up and get them back to the house before the storm broke. Sheila asked me to come too. She never liked being near Matt by herself. So we both went up. And we were just coming out from under the trees when we heard a cry."

He took a breath. Cally watched his profile and hardly breathed.

"Then, when we got past the cottage we could see the edge of the cliff. Matt stood there looking down. Just like in the picture. Next moment he turned and saw us and he yelled something about getting help. And then he ran to that place a little to the south of the tip — you know it — where you can get down through the trees. He went down that like a bat out of hell. I thought, later, that he wanted to make sure he got down before anyone else did." He looked at her. "Cally? You don't look so good."

"Just tell it, Noel."

"Well, Sheila ran back to the house to get help — she didn't know what had happened, but she had an inkling — and I followed Matt down the hill at a less suicidal speed. I found Francesca lying on the rocks at the base of the cliff, right under the stone face, obviously dead, and him crouched over her. He was babbling something like *Oh God help me*, and *What have I done*, and looking demented."

121

"What have I done...."

"Exactly. Of course the police questioned him. He said he was in the cottage, he'd gone in there to get some map or chart, he didn't see her fall, he just heard her cry out. He said he couldn't remember what he said when he found her. Said she was often not very careful, and he blamed himself for not making sure she stayed away from the edge of the cliff. The coroner ruled it was death by misadventure."

They sat in silence, side by side. At last Noel moved. He got to his feet and stood looking down at her. "Sheila and I always believed something different. I guess you've figured that out. But we weren't going to say so. Dad had his first major heart attack as soon as he got the news, and after that he was frail. The truth would have hurt him more. It might have killed him."

She pulled her wits together. "You never stopped to think Matt might have been telling the truth?"

"No, I didn't. Oh, I don't think he planned to kill her. I think he was simply in a rage, and lashed out."

"But why? What possible reason—"

"Oh, Cally." He held a hand down as if to help her up. She ignored it. "Cally, he was in love with her. It was written all over him, the way he looked at her. And she, well, she was young, too young for Dad. It was obvious they were having an affair. Maybe she tried to break it off." He hesitated and shrugged. "Well, that's the story. I'm sorry, Cally. You had to know."

He walked away. After a few minutes Cally got up, picked up her blanket, shook off the grass clippings and possible bugs, folded it and walked back to the house. She lay down in her room and waited for sleep to bring peace to her whirling brain and settle her sickened stomach, but peace never came.

Chapter 17

AT SIX O'CLOCK Cally put on a white sundress and went down to dinner. Noel, she thought, was no known flesh and blood. Despite the muggy heat, barely a trace of moisture showed on his smooth forehead. His light blue dress pants and snowy shirt were wrinkle-free. His tan leather wingtips were polished to a glassy shine. He smiled at Cally and looked pained when she failed to smile back.

Sheila had pulled her hair up into a pony tail and washed her hands but otherwise not made an effort to meet Noel's dress-for-dinner standards. Her shorts and halter top were still slightly damp, creased and smudged. Aubrey had put on clean clothes but still managed to look grubby, and he wasn't his usual airy self. Ginevra hadn't changed her dress in two days, and looked spectacular. Matt wasn't there. Cally wondered if he planned to sleep up at the cottage.

After dinner Mrs. Gardner brought iced tea and fresh lemonade to the terrace instead of coffee. Ginny stayed in the parlour and played *Brouillards* and other soft and moody pieces on the piano. Cally happened to be watching Aubrey watching Sheila, and so she saw Sheila's fingers tighten on her dripping glass. She followed her guarded glance. Matt had just emerged from the trees across the lawn and was walking toward the house.

He stopped at the base of the terrace steps and shot a glance at Cally, a flicker so brief she would have missed it if she hadn't been looking for it. Then his gaze skipped over Sheila and settled on Noel.

"I'm thinking of taking out one of the boats to get the canoe."

"Ah." Noel nodded.

"I don't want to drag the whole lake, though."

"Of course not."

"If someone were to come along and show me the place where it went down, I could try to pull it up."

The two of them sounded so civil, it was nerve-shattering. Cally wanted to jump up and yell. Sheila sat still as ice. Aubrey covered her free hand with his.

Noel shaded his eyes against the level sunshine. "You think there's enough time before sunset?"

"Just about, I'd say. I'd take the grapple hook from the boat-house."

"Right. It's on the shelf beside the float bags."

"The float bags?" Matt stared.

"Yes, you know. Inflatable things. Keep the canoe from sinking." Noel rocked a hand in the air. "The ones that were not in the canoe this morning."

"The ones that should have been. I put them in yesterday and I didn't take them out again." Matt's eyes flashed at Sheila. "We've been over this. Who'll help me find the place?"

Nobody answered. Then Aubrey gave Sheila's hand a pat and stood up. "I'll go."

THEY RETURNED in the twilight. "No luck," Aubrey said. He went into the house looking for Sheila, who had gone in to nurse a head-ache. Noel still occupied one of the deck chairs near the windows. Cally sat on the terrace balustrade, looking out over the lawn. They hadn't exchanged more than half a dozen words in the past hour. Matt took a seat one over from Noel, leaving an empty chair between them.

Ginevra had stopped playing the piano and now buzzed out onto the terrace. She rolled up on Matt's left. "I bet you're thirsty."

"Kinda."

"I'll take care of it!" She grabbed the empty pitcher from the table and rolled back into the house. Aubrey and Sheila passed her, walking hand in hand. They found seats behind the others.

The twilight deepened to its richest blue, to the point just before indigo. The air, perfectly still and perfumed with roses, was almost too heavy to breathe.

I hate you. I hate you, came the whisper.

Cally sat up straight and looked around, but neither Noel nor Matt had moved. Sheila sat with her eyes closed. Aubrey was leaning his chin on one fist. Nobody was saying anything. She glanced at the parlour windows. The room was brightly lit and empty.

"What's the matter?" Noel asked.

"Nothing." She sank down again.

Ginevra buzzed around the corner of the house, managing to convey bustle and fuss without altering her usual speed. She set a pitcher of iced tea on the table near Matt and held out a clean glass from the stack of them she had stuck in the carrier bag strapped to her armrest.

"Thanks, kidlet." Matt nudged her cheek with a knuckle.

"How did you manage all this?" Noel got up to help himself.

"Oh, no problem. There's lots of stuff I can do that people think I can't!" She poured helpings of iced tea and buzzed around handing them out.

Cally held the cold glass against her cheek, closed her eyes and listened to the ice cubes crack as they thawed. She wondered if she had a touch of fever. That would explain a lot.

I wish you were dead.

She looked around again. Nobody else seemed to have heard it.

125

And nobody was speaking except Ginevra, telling Sheila what new outfits she absolutely had to have before school started.

Cally slipped down from the balustrade and slowly, carrying her glass, strolled at a measured pace along the terrace, fighting the urge to run.

"Cally?" Noel said. "Off to bed so soon?"

"I, no, I just need to be inside. Too much sun, I think."

A sense of being stared at by unfriendly eyes sat on her shoulders until she turned the corner of the house and went in at the front door. Then it lifted and she breathed again.

"I heard it. I'm sure I heard it!"

The house was quiet. She climbed the stairs to the landing and sat down, still nursing her drink, although she no longer wanted it.

Think. What just happened?

Nerves. Nerves so roughly brushed up over the past five days that they were super-sensitive, like a cat's whiskers. That whisper had been feeling, not sound. But it had been as real as if someone had stood up and shouted it.

"But who? Oh God, I'm afraid. Why I am I still here?"

Well, there was Sheila, who maybe still needed her. And Ginevra. And there was.... *Cally, you fool.*

She sat breathing deeply and evenly, willing her heartbeat to stop jumping.

Footsteps sounded in the hall below. Sheila walked past the foot of the stairs and on into the kitchen. A light went on, spilling a yellow glow down the hall. "Cally?"

"Up here!"

Sheila came out of the kitchen and looked up the stairs. "What are you doing there?"

"I like stairs. They're calming and peaceful and high up. Good

126

for clear thinking."

"That's fine. You could do with some clear thinking."

"Couldn't we all?"

Sheila climbed the stairs and stopped a few steps down, so they were almost face-to-face. "Noel told me he talked to you this afternoon. About Matt. You must be feeling as if a piano fell on you. But—"

"But it was for my own good?"

"Well, yes."

"I'm not persuaded," Cally said quietly.

"What, after all you've been told?"

"Told? That's the catch. A lot's been said. Nothing's been proven."

"God!" Sheila threw her hands in the air. "Know something? You're living in a fairy tale, and I know which one — Beauty and the Beast. Come on, Cally, come back to the real world!"

She turned to start down the stairs. Cally caught her arm. "Wait! If you have any real evidence, you should show me! Why don't you?"

Sheila pulled her arm free. "Because I — Cally, we're friends. But there are things you don't know—"

"About Matt?"

"About me. Things I did."

"Things you did! But what—"

"Things that would make you hate me, if you knew. Things that could destroy me. So stop asking!" Sheila turned again, pushed past Cally and ran up the stairs.

Chapter 18

"CALLY! Is that you up there?"

Cally looked down to see Ginevra parked at the foot of the stairs, peering up at her.

"Yes, it's me," she said wearily.

"Then come down, I want to show you something." She swirled her wheelchair around and buzzed along the hall into the kitchen.

Cally groaned softly, stood up and came down the stairs. In the kitchen she emptied out the last of her drink, rinsed her glass, opened the refrigerator and poured a glassful of milk. Replacing the jug, she leaned against the fridge door and downed half the glass.

Then looked up to find Ginevra studying her. Ginny was sitting at the work table in the centre of the kitchen, resting her clasped hands on a large book that sat on the table in front of her.

"I'm not dumb, you know," she said. "I know what Sheila was so upset about, up there at the cottage."

"Um?"

"Yeah. She hates Matt. She doesn't trust him at all. I think she thinks he pushed my mother off the cliff — you know, she thinks he was in love with her, I heard her and Noel talking about it — they both think so — and they think he did something to Vanessa, too, but I can't figure out what."

"Gin," Cally began, not sure how much she should say, or how much Ginny already knew and understood. "All this is ancient history. And a lot of it is private. This really isn't something you should worry about, is it?"

"You bet it is! Sheila thinks he's like a bad old bear, and you know you can't ever trust bears even when they act tame, my dad said so once. He said bears are never really tame and you don't know what they'll do. So I want to show you something."

She held up the book. It was an album or scrapbook, the padded vinyl covers done in little-girl candy colours, pink and violet and silver, with hearts. "Sheila made this for me after my mother died." She flipped it open and riffled the plastic-sheathed pages full of photographs. "She printed out a whole bunch of pictures and put them in. I've put more things in myself since then. Here, sit down, you should see this."

Cally sat, and looked at the page Gin held open. Gin tapped it. "There, that's one of my favourites."

It was an eight-by-ten family photo taken on the island. George and Francesca sat on the terrace balustrade with Ginevra between them, their feet dangling above a flower bed, the house at their backs. Matt stood behind his father. There was a space next to him, and then Sheila and Noel close together.

"See how happy we look?" Gin waggled a hand. "Well, most of us, anyway."

Cally lingered over the picture. There was a lot to see. First to catch the eye, of course, were the three on the balustrade: Ginny a tiny wild-haired dynamo, swinging legs a blur; Francesca laughing down at her, one arm snug around her daughter, her own wild hair twisted up, her beauty even more alive and radiant than in the library portrait; and George, looking much younger than the 55 or 56 he must have been then, beaming at them both, one arm reaching to encircle his wife's shoulders.

Only two people were looking at the camera: Noel with a fixed smile, and Sheila with no smile. They both looked hardly more than children — they were just sixteen then, Cally figured after a moment — and Noel especially wore a brittle, fragile look. Sheila frowned defiantly. Matt was grinning down at his father and little Gin, his face lit with easy, happy affection. He must have been twenty then, and shining so in his young strength that Cally's heart twisted.

"And here's one of us after I had my fall." Ginevra flipped several pages over. "See, that's in Sick Kids Hospital. I was in there a long time. Daddy and Matt came to see me every single day. Sheila too," she said, as an afterthought.

This photo showed George and Matt sitting one on either side of a narrow hospital bed, with Ginevra propped up between them. George looked older than his years, here. Cally guessed his determined smile was put on for Gin's benefit. Matt, not smiling, a dark thundercloud in the midst of all that white, held one of Gin's small hands inside both of his large ones. Ginevra, thin and pale, beamed out at the camera like an inextinguishable candle flame.

"Did you know it was Matt who found me?"

"Found you?" Cally drew back and frowned at Ginevra. A cold knot formed in her stomach. *No. Please no.*

"After I fell," Ginevra supplied. "See, I liked being up there on the cliff, it was so wild and adventuresome, I used to pretend I was an explorer in the wilderness. So I went up there alone, a lot. And this time I thought I was alone, only I wasn't, and—"

"Gin, you don't have to talk about this. It must be upsetting."

"Oh, it doesn't bother me. It only bothers other people." Gin waved "other people" away. "Anyway, I fell down the face, but only about halfway down, on the nose, and then I slid down the nose and I landed on the mouth. You know how the top lip sticks out? That's where I ended up."

"Do you want to show me some other pictures?" Cally reached to turn the page, but Gin batted her hand away.

"Wait, I'm not finished. I started yelling, because I couldn't move, except my arms, and I was scared, and then, *yes!* Far, far away across the lake I saw a red boat, and then it got closer and I saw it was our red boat, and it was Matt! He'd been to the village. And he saw me waving and he came to my rescue!" Ginevra punched the air triumphantly and Cally laughed, warmth spreading through her. *Because of course he would never....*

"So he got the emergency guys there and they got me off, but it took a long time. And I started out being scared — I mean, right there on the lip of the stone face, like any second it would lick me off and *crunch* me! Can you imagine?"

"Yes. Yes, I can."

"But Matt was there the whole time and he protected me. He climbed down on a rope and he stayed by me and talked to me and kept me safe, and then I wasn't scared." She gazed at Cally with wide, insistent brown eyes. "Because he was my best brother and he loved me best and he still does. And that's how I know he's not a bear like Noel and Sheila think. He would never, ever hurt me, and I trust him—" She took a deep breath for emphasis. "—absolutely!"

They spent another fifteen minutes leafing through the album. Ginny, delighted by Cally's obvious interest, was lavish with details of where, what and when. "I took those myself, last spring before Daddy had his big heart attack. I have a camera that Sheila gave me." She tapped a picture of Matt moving rocks in a garden with George standing over him, pointing. Then one of George and Matt playing chess, both frowning down at the board, their facing profiles mirroring each other like two sides of a vase. A thought stirred at the back of Cally's mind and drifted forward.

"And this one I copied from the old album at home." Ginevra

flipped to the front to show a photo taped to the inside of the front cover. "I put it there because it comes before the others."

"But that's — No, wait." Cally held up the album to get a better light. The picture was a studio portrait. She'd thought at first that she was seeing Matt holding a baby and grinning delightedly at the camera over its head. But the woman sitting next to him, smiling firmly but without warmth, was unmistakably Julia, George's first wife.

"That's Matt when he was about a year old." Ginny smiled at it. "Wasn't he adorable?"

"But...." Cally's thoughts whirled. "He was adopted, wasn't he?"

"Yup, that's right."

So the man holding the dark-haired baby in that photo was George. Cally did a quick backwards count. He must have been about thirty-six then.

"He looks an awful lot like Daddy, doesn't he? I mean, Matt now looks a lot like Daddy looked then. I guess that's why they adopted him."

Cally glanced at Ginevra in surprise. At eleven, she must still be an innocent in many ways, and Cally wasn't about to enlighten her. She would work it out herself, given time.

"Done for now!" Ginny closed the album and slipped it carefully into her carrier. "I'll let you look at this again if you like, any time." With a cheerful wave she buzzed out of the kitchen. Cally sat staring blindly at the wall and working through the implications of what Gin had shown her.

An awful lot like? They might have been the same person. Or, more to the point, father and son. And judging by the pictures as a group, they had been close, those two. Closer, perhaps, than either of the twins had been to George. Their mother had made up for that, but their mother had not lived long. No wonder, perhaps, that Noel had set up Matt as his rival, and Sheila had been so quick to discover the bear in him.

Cally wondered who Matt's mother had been, and how the boy had come to live with his father. Had she died? Had she not cared about her little son? Or had she cared enough to let him go, to give him a chance at a better life? No way of knowing. Perhaps even Matt didn't know. She wondered if that unknown mother haunted him.

But how to reconcile what the twins believed Matt to be: betrayer of his own father and the next thing to a murderer, cruel, selfish, brutal — How to square that with the very different picture that emerged from Gin's album?

She was sure of two things, at least. Matt had loved his father and treasured their close relationship, and he'd never have done anything to put that at risk. And Ginevra had his heart. He would do anything to keep her from harm. The rest was a cloud of confusion.

Cally turned off the kitchen light and left the lower floor in darkness. She climbed to the second-floor corridor, where small shielded lights on the baseboards radiated a soft glow up the walls. Her feet made no sound on the carpet runner. At her door she paused, a hand on the knob. Farther along the corridor a bright patch on the carpet faded in and out. It was the fan of light from under Matt's door. She watched it darken, then reappear, then darken again. She pictured him pacing back and forth, back and forth, past his door.

The light flickered again, and now the shadow stayed. He must be standing near the door. Did he know she was out here watching? Was he waiting for her to speak? To knock?

While she was wondering, the light under Matt's door went out. Cally turned and went into her own room and closed the door.

Chapter 19

CALLY WOKE LATE and unrefreshed on Thursday morning. The previous twenty-four hours now seemed like one long bad dream, and it left a lingering sense of unease, the way a bad dream will.

Such a rash of unreasoning suspicion! She scowled into the mirror while sluicing her face with cold water and brushing her hair. There certainly had been something abnormal in the air, a kind of emotional poison, and they had all had been breathing it.

But no more. From now on, she would be objective. Her opinion of Matt, in particular, would be based on facts and common sense. Not on hearsay, suggestion or fantasy.

In this determined mood she went down to find breakfast in progress. Matt had finished early and gone up to the cottage. Noel was reading yesterday's copy of the *Globe and Mail* while nursing a second cup of coffee. Ginevra and Aubrey, as usual, were both polishing off second helpings of everything.

Sheila was breaking up a piece of toast with her fingers, not eating any of it. She avoided Cally's eyes. Cally thought of what Sheila had said last night on the stairs. "Things I did. Things that would make you hate me. Things that could destroy me."

She was almost certain that conversation had ended their friendship. And she would never know what those "things" were. And didn't want to know.

Cally had just lifted a forkful of hash browns to her mouth when Matt appeared in the doorway. He stood a moment in silence, his gaze travelling around the room as if taking inventory. Something in his fixed silence made Cally set down her fork and half-rise from her chair, than sink down again. Sheila's toast cracked and showered the table with crumbs.

Still in silence Matt circled the table to stand by Noel's chair. "Come with me," he said quietly.

"Why? Where?"

"The cottage. You'll see why."

"What happened?" Ginny's knife clattered on the table.

"Hush, Ginny." Noel slapped his newspaper down. "Can't it wait until I've finished breakfast?"

"No."

Matt's voice was colourless. His face was a mask. Aubrey looked across the table at Cally, eyebrows climbing into his hairline.

Noel frowned up at Matt. "Something bad, is it?"

"Yes."

"All right, then. Let's have a look." Noel drained his cup and pushed back his chair. "We might as well all go."

THE DOOR OF the cottage stood wide open. Matt, who had walked ahead, stood aside and jerked his head for the others to go in. As Cally passed him she looked up into his face, but the mask was still in place. His eyes swept over hers without any sense of contact. Then she heard Aubrey's "Holy shit!" and Ginny's gasp, and looking in she cried out in shock.

It was chaos. Floodlights were smashed, tools strewn about, panes of glass shattered. Lengths of lumber lay scattered. The wooden wall panels were deeply hacked again and again, the pale inner wood exposed like wounded flesh. The shutters, new and old, had been pried off their hinges and lay splintered on the floor. Worst, the roof beam was half chopped through from below. The axe was

135

still embedded in it.

The total effect was terrifying. Cally pictured somebody gone mad with rage.

In the midst of the mess, curled up like a spaniel in its basket, lay Jack Beamish, snoring. He held a whisky bottle and a mickey of rum, both empty, cradled lovingly in the crook of his arm.

Noel gazed around. "Good lord!"

"But the door was locked, wasn't it? So how—" Cally scanned the floor, then bent and picked up the padlock. One steel shank had been cut through. She handed it to Matt.

"Hacksaw." He tossed it aside with a clatter. His mask was slipping. He looked white and queasy, as if he'd just been kicked where it hurt most. And he had, Cally thought. She wanted to go to him, to take his hand, but he still hadn't looked at her as if he actually saw her. What was he afraid of, that she'd read something in his eyes? Something that would send her scurrying for safety?

He kicked aside the fragments of a shutter, then bent and picked up the hacksaw that had been hidden underneath. "Here it is. This is Jack's. I've seen him using it."

"So you think Jack did this?" Noel still gazed around, amazed.

Matt took a steadying breath. "Who else?"

"I don't know. But we shouldn't jump to conclusions. He could have wandered in here after the door was opened, after somebody else did the damage."

"But the hacksaw, Noel?" Cally put in.

"Might have been stolen," Sheila said abruptly. She had retreated to a spot near the door, as if ready to make a quick escape. "Easy enough. He keeps his tools in his room. Could be someone's trying to incriminate him. To get him fired." She met Matt's eyes defiantly. "We know how absurdly possessive he is about the cottage. He could

136

never have damaged it this way."

"Maybe you're right," Matt said quietly. "It's unlikely he would've done this cold sober. Or on his own."

"You think somebody put him up to it?" Aubrey put in.

"It's a possibility." Matt hadn't glanced at Aubrey. He held Sheila's eyes. "Hoaxes and tricks I expected. Mysterious lights, maybe the odd loosened stone, like last summer. But this? Why now, after thirty years on our payroll?"

Noel stepped in front of Sheila: a protective move. "Why indeed? I can't think of an answer, can you?"

"Maybe a whisper in his ear." Matt tilted his head. "A promise of money or free booze."

Noel stared. "You're really developing an obsession about poor old Jack, aren't you? Be careful, Matt. Be very careful."

"Come on, Gin." Sheila seized the back of Ginevra's chair and whirled it around. "You shouldn't be here. Out you go!"

"But I want to stay with Matt! I want to help!"

"No buts." Sheila pushed the chair, with difficulty (Cally guessed Gin was trying to apply the brakes) out the door and out of sight. Gin's furious cries faded into the distance.

Jack still snored, infuriatingly at peace, in the middle of the room. "Aubrey!" Noel beckoned. "Over here. Help me take Jack away. In the circumstances I don't think it wise or safe to let Matt lay hands on him."

"Oh, stuff it!" Matt bent to shake Jack by the shoulder. Noel moved as if to intervene, but stepped back when Matt straightened and flashed him a challenging look. Matt bent over Jack again. "Wake up!" he shouted in his ear.

Jack rolled over with a clinking of bottles, then suddenly sat up and stared wild-eyed at the circle of faces around him. He staggered to his feet. Then wavered as far as the doorway, where he slumped against the frame. His eyes drifted closed. Matt gripped him by one arm and led him, not roughly, onto the grass. Then he ducked back in, picked up the hacksaw and shoved it at him. "Yours?"

Jack blinked at it, then hugged it to his chest with a happy look. He turned left, then right, orienting himself, and marched raggedly away toward the trees.

The rest of them stood at the corner of the cottage and watched him go. Matt worked his shoulders, loosening tight muscles. He no longer looked like a tamped-down explosion, but he hadn't relaxed, either. Cally saw calculation in his eyes. "Noel," he said, in a measured conversational tone. "Question."

Noel put on a look of polite inquiry.

"For years now, and especially since Dad died, you've been soft on Jack. And this summer you've been letting him get away with murder. Like when he crashed the canoe. And that." He tipped his head back at the cottage. "Why?"

"I try to be fair, that's all."

"Oh, you're more than fair. Jack's had all the chances he deserves. Do the right thing and fire the bastard."

"But, Matt!" Noel spread his hands helplessly. "I can't fire him just like that. Oh, I know it looks bad. But we can't prove anything, can we?"

Cally stared at him, stunned. Could he be serious?

Matt studied the ground, hands in his jeans pockets, as if working out his next move. Then he turned away. "I guess I'd better sleep here tonight, then," he said over his shoulder. "There isn't much more he can wreck, but I wouldn't put it past him to try arson."

He was pushing up the sleeves of his sweatshirt as he headed back to the cottage.

Chapter 20

CALLY FOUND Ginevra in the parlour, angrily hammering the piano keyboard. "Lesson time!" Cally held up a stack of books and notebooks. Ginny growled and crashed the keys. Inwardly, Cally echoed her.

The morning spent on the terrace, as the sun sailed up the sky and the heat intensified, was a total loss as far as learning went. They both sighed with relief when Edna tapped on the parlour window and beckoned them in to lunch.

Matt did not appear for lunch or dinner, so after a silent and morose evening meal Cally went up after him, bringing a package of ham and egg sandwiches made by Mrs. Gardner. She found him inside the cottage, stacking the remains of his supply of lumber. It must have been his last chore, for the rest of the building was meticulously neat.

He looked up when she appeared in the doorway, and a smile lit his eyes. A knot loosened in her chest. She had been afraid he would still not want to know her.

"Looks like you worked non-stop all day."

The damage was still painfully visible, though. The broken shutters stood in a row against one wall. The wall panels were still gouged and splintered. Matt had nailed together lengths of lumber to make four-by-fours, and two of these supports had been wedged under the hacked roof beam.

"Work's great for keeping the horrors in the back corners where they belong," he said.

She didn't ask what horrors, just held out the packet. "Hungry?"

"And thirsty." He stretched his arms and shoulders, then pulled two cans of juice from the cooler and led the way out of the cottage. The evening was sultrier than ever, but at least out here you could feel the air move a little.

They sat down on the cliff edge, almost knee to knee, and shared juice and sandwiches. Matt gazed out wearily over the lake, where a rose-peach sky was reflected. The water looked rusty. Haze hid the horizon.

"Are you still planning to stay up here for the night?" she asked at last.

"You bet."

"But why? After all Jack's done, surely he wouldn't—"

"Sure he would. He's capable of any crazy thing." He added, "Or somebody is."

"What does that mean?"

He looked at her, opened his mouth to speak, frowned, and looked away. He was suddenly a thousand miles distant again.

Over his shoulder she saw the cottage, squat and secretive. "How I hate that thing!"

"What?" He looked around in surprise.

"That pile of stone. It's so ugly and cold. I can really believe there's something in there, something horrible that feeds on misery. Nothing good ever happened in that cottage or near it!"

Matt's tight face relaxed into a grin. "Well, there's our answer. All of us have been in and out of that place since we were kids. Even Sheila. It's been working its baleful influence on us all these years. So, yeah, we can blame it all on the cottage!"

"Don't laugh. It's not a good place. Sheila's right about that."

"You seriously think it's haunted?"

"I don't believe in ghosts. But if I did, yes, it would definitely be haunted."

"Funny, Francesca never reacted at all to the cottage. She wasn't sensitive to atmosphere, I guess. A lot like Gin, in that way. She used to come up here a lot."

She couldn't stop herself. "You loved her, didn't you?"

He turned his head and looked straight into her eyes. "Yes. I did."

Oh God. Why can't I keep my big mouth shut?

He turned back to gaze out over the lake, arms clasped over his knees. She thought that was it, and she might as well get up and go. Then he stirred and said, "She was nineteen when Dad brought her home and — well, you saw her portrait. And me? Cally, I was *fifteen*. Of course I was in love! Desperately, achingly, head over heels." He laughed a little, fondly amused at his younger self. "She handled it just right. Light and laughing but not making fun of me. And after a year or so I grew out of that and then I just ... just loved her. I loved her warmth, her sweetness — I know, old-fashioned word, but it was true. And her courtesy to everyone, even the disgusting Jack. I loved her devotion to Dad. I loved the way she adored little Ginny. Everybody loved her."

Listening to his voice, watching the flicker of memories across his face, Cally was sure of one thing. He had never harmed Francesca. *He knows how to love, and how to lose, without hurting anyone but himself.* And she knew it was too late for her to corral her heart now.

"Not everybody," she murmured.

"You're right, Noel and Sheila never accepted her. That hurt her. I think they always saw Francesca as Dad's mid-life mistake, another intruder — like me." He sighed. Then quietly he said, "You don't need to be afraid of Francesca, Cally."

"I think I know that now."

He lifted one hand and brushed back a strand of hair that kept floating into her eyes. "Remember how you said nothing good ever happened in the cottage? I can think of one thing."

"What?"

"It happened Tuesday. Two days ago. You said you cared about ... about me. Oh, and Sheila too." His fingertip traced the curve of her cheek. The icy spot inside her melted.

"I don't recall getting feedback." Her voice was husky.

"And you won't, not now."

"Why not?"

He went back to clasping his knees. "I said then that you should go away. Seems to me I've said that before, more than once. If I asked again, would you go?"

"No."

"Right. Well, now I'm almost glad. Because I need you to help keep an eye on Ginny. I don't like the way things are going."

"You've said that before. Which way are things going?"

His mouth set. "Badly. If only I could go away myself, but—"

"Why can't you?"

"Because of Gin. She shouldn't be here. But Noel won't see that she should leave — yes, I've raised the issue — and so long as Gin's here I can't leave. And so this thing that's coming — I'm afraid there's no stopping it."

She touched his arm. Wished he would unwrap it from his knees and wrap it around her instead, and pull her close. "Will you ever explain?"

"Oh, yes, someday. When all this is settled." He flexed his shoulders again. "But meantime, you'd better keep clear of me."

"What — am I crowding you?" She scrambled to her feet.

142

"Hey! Sit down!" He caught her hand and pulled her down again. "I wish you would crowd me." His mouth bent up, lopsided. "But just now, I'm risky company. What was it somebody said about the poet Byron? 'Mad, bad, and dangerous to know.' That's me." He let go of her hand and faced front again.

Cally stared out over the rust-coloured lake. The sun was going down into a reddish haze. The wind brought an aromatic scent. She sniffed. "Mm. Smells like incense."

"Forest fires," Matt said. She looked at him, startled, and he nodded. "That's pine resin burning. Don't worry, it's nowhere close. It's miles north of here." He sounded untroubled, but she couldn't stop a shiver of apprehension.

If they were the only two people in the world, how simple things would be! But they weren't. There were Sheila, and Noel, and Ginny, and even Aubrey. And Jack, too. Their several lives twisted together like the strands of a fuse. And all it needed was one good spark to set it smouldering toward an explosion.

Chapter 21

MATT CAME BACK to the house to get a sleeping bag and left again. Cally went up to her room, sat on her balcony and tried to read. Night fell. She closed the book, tracked the circling nighthawk by its cries and watched the light of the cottage shining through the trees. The light winked out after less than an hour.

That night she lay endlessly awake on her sweat-dampened sheets, listening to the soft creak of the ceiling fan. She wondered if Matt was asleep now in his uncomfortable bedroll, or if he was as wakeful as she was. She prayed Jack would have the sense to stay in his own room.

Cally longed for morning. And she dreaded it.

Her eyes closed for what seemed only a moment. When they opened again, the gloom was tinted pink. Rosy light outlined the curtains. She lay wondering what had wakened her. Some noise? A few sleepy chirps betrayed sparrows disturbed in their roosts under the eaves.

The noise came again. A series of impatient bangs, and a voice calling. She rolled off the bed and seconds later was out in the corridor, sashing her robe. Noel was on his way down the stairs.

Now there were voices in the hall below. Sheila's door opened. "Who's that?" The two of them ran barefoot down the stairs. Mrs. Gardner followed slowly, groaning a little with stiffness.

Noel stood at the open door facing a man in uniform. The flash on his shoulder said OPP. Cally was suddenly hyper-alert. Sheila's hand closed on her wrist.

The officer's eyes flicked from face to face. "Is everybody here?"

"Most of us," Noel said. "What's the trouble? Don't tell me —
more vandalism?"

"Bit more than that. There's a man lying dead on the rocks at the
other end of your island."

Cally reached out her other hand and clung to the newel post of
the stairs. Her heart gave one heavy thud, and after that a vast silence
spread out around her like ice on a pond. She saw Matt's face shattered.

Nothing moved. Nobody spoke. The officer seemed to stand frozen, his mouth partly open. The air thickened in front of her eyes.

Then babel broke out. Over the confusion only the policeman's
voice rose clear. "Yes, I'm sure. I ran my boat in and examined him.
Looks like he fell from the cliff above."

"Who...." Cally heard her own voice as if it belonged to somebody else.

"I'm new to the area; don't know him. No ID on him. Weathered
skin. Age, I'd say, in the late fifties."

"Jack!" Noel's eyes flashed bright blue. Cally hugged the newel
post, her knees liquid. Sheila whispered something and turned away.

"Poor Jack!" Mrs. Gardner twisted her hands together. "I knew
the bottle would finish him, one way or another."

"We can't assume anything yet," the officer said. "I'll take my
boat straight back there. I've called for backup. Will one of you come
out to identify him, please? Just one. We don't want a crowd."

"Matt!" Cally felt a rush of urgency. "Somebody should go to the
cottage and tell him."

"I expect he already knows," Noel murmured. "But I'll go. I'll
take a boat round."

"There was somebody in the cottage?" The officer looked interested.

Just then Aubrey came yawning and blinking down the stairs, and Ginny buzzed out of her elevator, bright-eyed and excited. "What's happening?" she demanded.

There was a flurry of reassuring voices. Ginny shook her tangled curls as if being attacked by gnats. "Just tell me!" Then, "Oh no! Matt!" and seemed for a moment to half-rise from her chair, as if levitated by anxiety.

"Not Matt!" Cally said quickly. "It's Jack. He got hurt. Matt is fine."

"I have to go to him!" Ginny headed at top speed for the front door. Noel caught the wheelchair before it could crash into the officer's knees.

"No, you don't! You don't leave this house today, you hear?"

Ginny shot him a look, then swivelled her chair to face Cally. "You'll have to go."

"No, Cally won't—" Noel began.

"Yes, Cally will," she said, and went back to her room to pull on whatever clothes came to hand.

WHEN SHE ROUNDED the corner of the cottage she found Matt in a position that looked familiar: feet apart, on the brink of the cliff, looking down. She recalled Sheila's painting. The memory was disturbing. She pushed it away. He glanced back over his shoulder as she approached.

"Looks like you've been up awhile," she said. His dark hair was brushed back damply, his face stubbly but alert. He wore a fresh sweatshirt and yesterday's jeans.

"Not that long."

"How did it happen?"

"Beats me," he said in a colourless voice. "Looks like he fell."

She peered over the cliff edge. Noel had beached his boat several yards away along the shore, and was standing as far from the scene as possible. He was trying not to look at the sprawled figure on the rocks, but his eyes kept sliding back to it. Cally's heart choked her throat. She was glad she wasn't any closer to the scene.

At the base of the cliff, a uniformed policeman was making notes while a grey-haired man in plain clothes bent over Jack's body. A doctor, Cally guessed. The officer who had hammered on their door stood nearby, holding a camera. Two police launches were drawn up on the beach beyond Noel's boat.

The first man put away his notebook and let his gaze travel slowly up the cliff, as if measuring its height. Seeing the two standing at the top, he waved them back.

"I guess he doesn't want us messing up the evidence." Matt walked away from the edge. Cally followed.

"Evidence?" She went cold.

"He probably fell from just about here." He nodded at the cliff edge where they'd been standing.

"But it was an accident, wasn't it?"

"Of course it was." He didn't sound convinced.

"Look at the edge. One of the boulders is gone." The missing rock had left a deep gouge in the lip of the cliff. "Jack must have been standing on it, and it fell." She turned to him eagerly. He shook his head.

"I had a good look down there. It looks more as if he fell first, then the rock landed on top of him."

Didn't need to know that! How could Matt be so calm?

He raised his head, listening to the rustle and scuff of climbers on the less-sheer, shrubby southwest face of the cliff. Noel reached the

147

top first, followed by a tall man with a clipped reddish mustache. It was Sergeant Ed Borrows. Cally remembered seeing him in the detachment office at Port Devon.

"Well, sir. I understand you spent the night in the cottage. Happen to hear anything?" His voice was bland; his eyes, fixed on Matt's, were sharp.

"No, nothing disturbed me. I slept from ten till just after dawn."

"So you slept right through the noise of the officer's boat?"

"I'm a very heavy sleeper. I sleep like the dead." Matt's tone was light and he met the officer's eyes steadily. But Cally could feel waves of tension radiating from him. He stood poised, like a man ready for a fight.

"Not quite like the dead." Borrows flicked a glance toward the cliff. "Would you three go into the cottage, please, and shut the door?"

"Why?" Matt's brows twitched downward.

"Humour me. Got any objection?"

Cally slid a hand through Matt's taut-muscled arm and nudged him toward the cottage. Noel followed. Once the door was shut she had trouble breathing. More than ever before, the air in this place felt thick with a presence, something that had fattened on the night's bloodshed.

Through one narrow window she watched Borrows as he walked to the edge of the cliff, keeping away from the gouged place. He picked up a stone and tossed it out. They heard the crack and thud of its fall. Then he called, "Hey!" and started back toward the cottage. Noel opened the door for him.

"Hear anything?" asked the sergeant.

"We heard you call," Noel said. "Plainly."

He looked at Matt. "You, sir?"

"I heard you."

"And the stone, you heard that?"

"Yes."

"And yet you heard nothing last night?"

"Not a thing. Like I said."

"Maybe," Cally ventured, "there was nothing to hear?"

"Maybe." The man's eyes never left Matt's face.

"I, uh." Noel smiled weakly. "I presume you're going to take statements from us."

"We'll want to talk to everybody on the island." Borrows moved his eyes to Noel. "You have something you want to say?"

"Perhaps. But I'd prefer to say it privately."

Cally knew what he had to tell. An account of yesterday's vandalism and Matt's reaction to it would not go down well.

Matt knew it too. He sent Noel a humourless smile. Borrows didn't miss that either, Cally thought.

The officer faced Matt. "Looks like we're about finished here, for now. I'd like you, Mr. Forrest, to come back with me to the detachment office."

"Is this an arrest?"

"No, I'd just like to run over a few details with you."

"And if I say no?"

"Sir, things'll go a lot smoother for all of us, including yourself, if you'll co-operate."

Wonderfully courteous, Cally thought. And about as soft as the granite under their feet.

Under her fingertips, Matt's tense forearm suddenly relaxed. "Why not?" He gently set her hand aside and followed Borrows out of the cottage.

WHEN HE CAME out of the detachment office in Port Devon Cally was waiting for him, standing in front of the window of the tackle shop, her eyes fixed on the station door. It was nearly noon, and she'd been there for half an hour. She'd changed into a clean pair of jeans and one of her prettier T-shirts, heliotrope with sequins, for all the good that would do. At least he wouldn't see her looking a wreck.

He crossed the street, trying to return her smile, but not doing a very good job of it. "How did you get here?"

"A policeman came to the house to question us, then he drove me here in one of our boats. It's down at the marina." She pointed. "Mrs. Gardner took the other boat and ferried Edna to Blackwater Bay."

"You mean the troops have deserted?"

"Just Edna. She's scared, Matt. Not Mrs. Gardner, though. She says people still need meals and clean beds, even in the midst of death and destruction."

"Good ol' Mrs. G!" He took her hand and swung it. They started toward the marina. "So the officer took statements from everybody?"

"Yes. I told him what happened at the cottage yesterday. I described how restrained your behaviour had been, just in case Noel forgot to mention that in his statement."

"Do you think I killed Jack?"

She looked up, aghast. His eyes flickered with what might have been fear or despair.

"No! Of course not!"

"There's a but in there somewhere."

"Well, you haven't told me everything, have you? You're holding something back."

"Nothing but guesses. And the less you know the better."

That wasn't near good enough, but Cally's antennae told her it was the best she was going to get. "Where to now?"

"Back to the island. As ordered."

"But they've let you go. Doesn't that mean they believe you?" Her attempt at optimism was fraying.

He gathered her into the curve of his arm. "I'm not in handcuffs yet. They did ask if I pushed Jack over, then heaved a rock on top of him—"

"Oh God!"

"I said no. Then Borrows took me over the same ground again, very politely and correctly. He also mentioned the coincidence of two fatal falls — Francesca and Jack — in almost the same spot, and me the only other person there each time. He asked me to comment."

"Matt—"

"Not to worry. I said I couldn't have been the only other person there last night, unless Jack pushed himself off. Because I didn't do it. Anyway, there were no floodlights or truncheons. But it was thorough. The man knows his job."

She shivered. "I'm afraid of him."

"I would be, if I were guilty. Come on, let's get back."

Directly overhead, the sun glinted like a tarnished dime. A yellow haze stained the sky. Cally sniffed the air as they walked. The incense of burning pine forests was stronger. From now on, that scent would forever be linked in her mind with a sense of dread.

151

Chapter 22

IT SEEMED ludicrous to carry on as normal when nothing felt normal, but what else was there to do? After landing at the pier on Stone Face Island, Matt announced that he would begin repairing the damage done to the panelling in the cottage. When Cally offered to help, he shook his head. "Remember what I said? Mad, bad, and dangerous to know. Keep clear. And keep an eye on Gin." He smiled, but there was nothing soft in his face.

Cally spent most of the afternoon bobbing about in the lake, the one cool place she could find. Sheila sat on a big flat boulder under the trees near the beach, sketching. A tinkle of piano music drifted from the house. Noel retreated to the library and barricaded himself behind stacks of paperwork. Business was his castle keep, Cally thought, just as work on the cottage was Matt's.

Late in the afternoon she sank with a tired sigh onto the other half of the rock where Sheila sat. The stone was blood-warm. She towelled her dripping hair and squinted up at the haze-dulled sky.

"It's going to be another sticky night."

"I wish the storm would break now." Sheila didn't look up from her sketch pad.

"You and me both." Cally felt like an over-strung guitar. The threatening storm wasn't to blame, but it wasn't helping.

"I wish we could leave," Sheila said. "If only the police would get a move on!"

The police had asked them to stay on the island for a while. "Even if I could leave, I couldn't." Cally meant Matt and Gin. And,

152

yes, Sheila, although there was no point in saying so now.

"Our only hope is that they get this wrapped up quickly." Sheila held up her sketch pad. "Can't imagine why they haven't arrested him yet."

She'd sketched Matt's face. It was the face of a killer.

"Sheila—"

"We all know what happened last night." Sheila set the pad back on her knee and added a touch more charcoal above the eyes, deepening their menace.

"Do we? I don't. All I know is, Matt wouldn't kill Jack. Oh, he had good reason to be tearing-mad, but he wouldn't lose control like that. I've seen him furious with Jack before this and he was never more than a little rough."

"Suppose he had a stronger motive than you think?"

"Such as?"

"Blackmail."

Cally tried to laugh. "What on earth could Jack know that would push Matt that far? You've got to admit Matt has guts enough to say publish and be damned."

Sheila studied her sketch of him. "Yes, he has guts. He also has a temper. Can't you see him surprising Jack in the night, catching him on the cliff edge? Losing his temper, hitting out. Maybe when he realized what he'd done, he was sorry. Maybe. I can see all that happening. Can't you?"

The picture was so vivid in Cally's mind that for a moment she could see nothing else. Then that vision faded and another came into focus. Matt's face, guarded as any fortress, dense with firepower. But all that power checked and disciplined.

"No. I can't."

Sheila slapped her sketch pad shut. "Are you absolutely, one hundred percent sure of him? Beyond a shadow of a doubt?"

"I'm not one hundred percent sure of anybody. Not even myself." Cally got up, slung her wet towel over her shoulder, and started up the path to the house.

Noel appeared at the top, still impossibly neat in tailored button-up shirt and crisp cotton pants. "Is Ginevra with you?" he called. "It's getting near dinner time, and I can't find her."

Sheila stood up. "Isn't she with Aubrey?"

"She was until half an hour ago. Then she went to her room. Or at least," he added carefully, "Aubrey says she said she was going to her room."

Cally glanced west, toward the cliff end of the island. Toward the cottage. Sheila caught the glance and drew in her breath. "I told her not to go there! Noel, would you go up?"

He looked unwilling, but he nodded. Cally said, "I'll go too." He shot her a grateful smile and captured her hand as they set off together. As they crossed the lawn toward the woods she pulled free, gently but with finality.

It was not that she disliked Noel. She used to like him quite a lot. But after seeing him at close quarters for nearly a week, he wasn't the person she'd thought he was. He was less kind, less balanced, less civilized. As they walked single-file up the stone-dust path through the woods she felt his cool presence behind her like a breath on the back of her neck.

"Cally," he said. "Cally, remember. If anything ever goes wrong, if you need me, I'm here."

She looked over her shoulder. "What do you mean, if anything goes wrong?"

He smiled briefly. "Nothing now. Just keep it in mind."

Nobody was in sight when they emerged from the woods and

crossed the tussocky meadow toward the cottage. Voices came to them: at first only sounds, no words. Matt's deep voice, then Ginevra's eager piping. Then a clatter and "Oops! Sorry!" from Ginny.

They rounded the corner of the cottage and Cally stopped short. Noel bumped into her and gripped her arm. An empty wheelchair sat outside near the open door. Noel made an urgent sound, set Cally aside and took three quick steps across the threshold. He stopped there, blocking her view. She pushed at him and felt him trembling with some strong emotion, something she couldn't interpret. She pushed again and he stepped aside.

"Good lord in heaven," she said softly.

For a moment nobody moved. Matt, a screwdriver in hand, knelt on the floor with one knee on a shutter. He had half-turned and was looking at Noel.

Ginevra stood beside him holding a large iron hinge. That had to be what had made the clatter: she'd dropped the hinge. Her face slowly flushed to a deep red.

"You're standing up," Cally said wonderingly.

"It was — ah—" Ginny gasped. "Stress! The stress of the moment!" Her face lit with a look of awe. "It's a miracle!"

Cally remembered a few things. The empty wheelchair on the cliff edge. Ginny nearly springing out of the chair this morning, when she feared Matt was in trouble. Her "no problem" getting the iced tea the other night.

"Miracle shmiracle," Cally said. Ginny started to giggle. Matt, who had been watchfully silent, broke into a grin. Cally felt a spring of astonished laughter rising inside. But then Noel stepped forward and she got a look at his face, and the laughter died.

"How long," he said quietly, looking down at Matt, "have you known about this?"

Matt rocked back off his knees and stood up, taking his time. He took the hinge from Ginny's hands. "Since Tuesday evening," he answered pleasantly.

"And you kept it to yourself?"

"I thought it best."

Noel held his gaze a moment. Then he looked at Ginny, who had stopped giggling and was biting her lips nervously. "How long have you been lying to us?"

"Lying! No!" She blazed up, then wavered. "I never lied, not really. I just, um, never said." She stifled more giggles.

"Then I think you have some *saying* to do." He held out an open hand toward the doorway. "Back to the house. We'll all need to hear this."

Ginny shrank back against Matt. He patted her shoulder. "Not to worry, kidlet. I'll be there."

"No need, Matt," Noel said.

"Oh, I think there is need. No, Cally, leave the wheelchair, I'll bring it down later."

Chapter 23

THE STORY CAME out in the parlour. They were all there: Sheila still vibrating with shock, silent after her first outburst, sitting on the sofa and gazing at Ginny with hungry eyes. Aubrey beside her, one long hand covering her clasped hands, his mobile face twitching with barely suppressed laughter. Mrs. Gardner standing hands-on-hips in the doorway, dumbfounded and troubled. Noel silent and grim, as if from a betrayal. Matt leaning on the piano, watchful, unreadable.

And in the middle: Gin, sitting on the piano bench facing outward, swinging her legs back and forth and glorying in their freedom. She looked smug, nervous and embarrassed.

Noel had reminded everyone that as Gin's guardian he, and he alone, had the right to question her. "All right," he said now, feet planted, arms crossed, staring down at her. "Let's have it. How long have you been hoaxing us?"

"There was no hoax," Matt said heavily. "You know that. The doctors tried everything."

"I'm asking her, not you." Noel kept his gaze on Gin. She met it defiantly.

"Since just after last Thanksgiving."

"What happened then? Suddenly you could walk?"

"You don't believe me, but this is true." She looked past him at Sheila. "It was at my school. I was in bed and one night I could feel a little something in my right big toe. I thought I was imagining it but I kept feeling it, and I tried moving it, and then one day it did move — just a little." She bounced on the bench and broke into a smile. "I

157

almost told then, but I decided not to."

"But Ginny, why not?" Sheila's voice broke on the last word.

"Don't you see, I wanted to do it myself!" Gin spread her arms wide. "I had this wonderful plan. It would have to be at home, and Christmas would be too soon, but I knew I had until summer, at least. And then one day you'd call me to dinner and I'd come sailing down the stairs in a blaze of glory! Think how amazing that would be!"

"Oh, Gin," Sheila murmured.

"Besides, I knew if I told, Noel would have doctors at me night and day, poking and testing, and all that boring therapy. I hate doctors! So — I cured myself." She tossed her curls back and smiled with immense self-satisfaction.

"You didn't cure yourself, you silly little twit!" Aubrey was grinning. "You were incredibly lucky you healed as well as you did. But how did you do it?"

"I just kept at it, trying to move my toes, then my feet. I worked upward. I got horrible cramps, but I knew those were a good sign. I got books about it — there's loads of them in the school library. That part took till nearly Easter. Nobody knew except my roommate, and she swore to keep it secret. When I could move my legs I borrowed her walker and every spare minute, I exercised. Then after school finished and we came to the island, I'd go outside after everybody else was in bed. I'd sneak down the back stairs and out the kitchen door and I'd go down to the beach and walk and walk and walk. And that's it." She rocked back and forward on the piano bench, smiling. "It's only been three months, really, since I could walk more than a few steps on my own. And see me now!"

She hopped off the bench and pranced across the room. She spun around and balanced on one foot. She swept a graceful bow and came up radiant. It was her moment of triumph, thin white legs and grubby shorts and all.

What a scene, Cally thought. The day had brought death and police and disaster and the threat of storm, and here in this room,
watching this vain, beautiful little girl, all that shrunk to unimpor-
tance. Aubrey was shaking his head and laughing. Sheila was gazing
with tears on her cheeks. Noel stood frowning at Gin, as if she was a
puzzle he was trying to work out.

Matt wasn't watching Gin. He was watching everybody else. His
eyes met Cally's and he nodded almost imperceptibly. Implications
trickled into Cally's mind.

Noel held out both hands as if to subdue a noisy crowd. "Gin.
You made a habit of going out at night, secretly?"

"Well, I had to. It was the only way I could exercise."

"Never mind. Did you go out last night?"

"Yes. For a while."

"Did you go anywhere near the cottage?"

"I was there," Matt put in. "She didn't."

"You might have been asleep. Gin: I'm asking you. Did you go
near the cottage?"

She shrugged and looked away. "Maybe. I did sometimes."

"Last night?"

"Maybe."

"Did you see Jack?"

She laughed. "I liked to follow Jack! He was always talking to
his great-granddad. Really weird! Sometimes I made noises and he
thought I was a ghost!"

"Oh, Gin," Sheila whispered. "Don't you know how dangerous
that could've been?"

"Sheila, hush," Noel said. "Gin, look at me."

She looked at him, her large brown eyes unblinking.

"Did you see Jack near the cottage last night?"

"I, well, not exactly. He was more near the cliff. He was talking to somebody. But it was dark and they were near some bushes so I didn't really see."

Sheila sat up and her eyes went to Matt. Matt pushed away from the piano.

"Gin," Noel said. "Did you hear what they were saying?"

"No. I couldn't make it out. It was too far. I just knew it was Jack and somebody else."

"Did you see the other person?"

"No, I already said!"

Noel took a breath. "Ginny, listen. You know what happened to Jack, don't you?"

Her gaze wavered. Cally longed to go and put an arm around her. For all her nerve and attitude, Gin was very childlike just then.

"Did you see what happened, Gin?"

"No! I didn't see anything. I was tired. I went away."

Thank God. But then: were Gin's eyes slightly veiled, was her voice a tone too glib?

"Ginevra." Noel set his hands on her shoulders and stared into her eyes. "Are you lying?"

"No!"

Matt's hands fisted; then opened as if forced.

"If you know anything — anything at all — you must tell me. This is serious."

"I've already told you everything!"

"The police will be back soon, perhaps tomorrow. Would you rather talk to Sergeant Borrows?"

"No, 'cause I don't know anything. I *told* you!"

"All right." He sighed, and released her. "But no more running

160

about at night until this situation is cleared up. Do you hear?"

"Yes," she muttered.

The group broke up. Gin was the first to go, skipping out of the room in a burst of relief and pent-up excitement. Mrs. Gardner swept a disapproving look around the room, Cally wasn't sure why, then went back to the kitchen shaking her head. Noel sat down beside Sheila and took her hands. He stabbed a look at Aubrey, dismissing him. Aubrey lifted his eyebrows and sat back, but he didn't go away.

Cally found Matt on the terrace. He was laughing down at Ginevra, who was demonstrating her awesome new agility by turning cartwheels on the lawn. Only, the cartwheels kept collapsing in a flurry of arms and legs.

She touched his arm. "What d'you think? Did she see anything?"

"Not sure." He kept his eyes on Gin. "If only— But that's Gin all over, as biddable as a cat. When I found out on Tuesday night, I told her not to roam. I was afraid she might be spotted."

"And then what?"

"I'm not even sure myself. It just felt damned unsafe."

"And now you're worried. Not about what she might have seen, so much as what somebody thinks she might have seen."

He nodded. "And we—"

He cut that off as Gin came dancing across the lawn and up the terrace steps. She flung herself at him in an extravagant hug. "It's just so glorious! Now I don't have to hide!"

"Yeah, glorious." He held her off and scowled at her. "You promise not to roam around alone after this?"

"Promise!" She beamed back at him.

"Cross your heart? I'm serious, now."

She drew herself up and solemnly crossed her heart.

"All right. And remember what I said, eh? About...." He narrowed his eyes in a significant way. Gin's expression went inward. She nodded, subdued. "Otherwise, when I'm not here," he added, "rely on Cally."

Gin's eyes flicked at Cally and she nodded again. Then she slipped free and danced back onto the lawn.

"Secrets," Cally said.

"I hope not for long." Matt carried a chair to the top of the steps and settled into it. He pulled out the battered pack of cigarettes, got one out and sat fingering it, unlit, and watching Gin. Cally sat beside him until dinnertime.

DINNER WAS SERVED at six-thirty exactly. Cally kept thinking of the mad tea party in *Alice in Wonderland*, such an air of unreality filled the room. They were all there, all pretending to enjoy the meal on which Mrs. Gardner had spent all her talents, but Cally doubted that anyone except Ginny tasted a tenth of what went down.

Matt and Noel sat at opposite ends of the table and, across the snowy linen, the glittering crystal and gleaming silver and china, engaged in a conversation so neutral it crackled with things unsaid. They talked pleasantly of food, and the carpet business, and Matt's current architectural project. They talked with concern about the drought and the danger of forest fires. Matt joked with Ginevra and addressed impersonal remarks to Cally, who felt her face go cardboard-stiff in the effort to smile.

Sheila was silent, only flicking a glance at Gin from time to time, eating nothing and drinking only water. Aubrey watched Sheila and spoke at random, with none of his usual sparkle.

Since Mrs. Gardner had lost her helper, after dinner Cally and Ginevra cleared the table. Ginny darted about fetching and carrying with more élan than skill, but nothing was broken. Then Cally offered

162

to help with the dishes, but Mrs. Gardner shooed her away and asked her to carry out the after-dinner drinks instead.

On the terrace the air of unreality persisted. Cally sat nursing her drink and listening to Noel and Matt blandly remarking on the heat.

Sheila, unusually restless, moved erratically about the house and grounds. After a while Cally realized her movements were not erratic at all.

Ginny was very mobile this evening, enjoying her new ability to move about freely. When she went back into the kitchen to scrounge a second helping of ice cream, Sheila waited for her in the hall. When Gin took her ice cream and sat beside Matt on the terrace, Sheila watched them from a window. When Gin announced that she was going for a swim, Sheila waited a few minutes and then followed, quietly but openly.

Cally made sure that she, too, was on the beach for the half hour Gin spent splashing about in the shallows. Sheila sat on the pier sketching, seemingly oblivious of everyone else. But when Ginevra went back up to the house, Sheila went too, a minute later.

Increasingly aware of being watched, Gin grew nervous and snappish and finally said that she was going up to bed — "So I can have some time to myself!" Sheila watched her run upstairs, but to Cally's relief, did not follow. Instead she curled up on the sofa in the parlour and listened to Aubrey coaxing Gershwin tunes from the piano.

The music floated through the window to the terrace, where the brothers still sat an arm's length apart, gazing out over the lawn and trees to the lake. "Quite a sunset," Noel said. Matt placidly agreed.

Quite a sunset. In the west the sun had melted into a sea of blood. Cally thought of burning forests and bleeding wounds. *I can't stand any more of this.* "Goodnight. I'm off to bed," she said. Both brothers answered: Noel with a smile, Matt briefly.

Before going into her own room she looked in on Ginevra, whose door was directly across from hers in the corridor. Gin was lying on her bed, stomach down, feet hooked together and swaying in the air. She was reading a shabby-looking hardcover.

"That looks like an original Nancy Drew," Cally said.

"It's not, but it's sort of like that. It's a real old one out of the library downstairs. Pretty cool." Gin held it up to show the torn dustcover. It was *The Mystery of the Twin Corpses.*

Cally laughed and wished her sweet dreams. She was about to leave when she noticed that there was no lock on the door. "Gin?" She pointed.

"Oh, that! Daddy had that taken off years ago, after my accident. He was afraid I might have a fall while I was in my room with the door locked."

Cally hesitated, not wanting to scare the girl. Then decided not to take a chance. "Want to have a sleepover in my room? You'd be comfy, it's a big bed. And I just might be able to smuggle up some chocolate biscuits!"

"No, s'okay." Ginny looked up, mildly irritated. "I know what Matt said but I don't need babysitting every single minute! Besides, Mrs. Gardner's right next door." She tilted her head at the wall.

"Mrs. Gardner?" That room, the one closest to the back stairs, had been empty. Mrs. Gardner's usual room was on the third floor. "She moved down? When?"

"After dinner. If I need anything all I have to do is pound on the wall. So you see, I'll be *just fine.*"

"Well, if you do need anything, don't just pound on the wall. Shout for me and Matt, too."

"I will." Ginevra mimed longsuffering patience, a wrist on her

164

brow. As an afterthought she added, "Thanks."

In the corridor once more, Cally looked toward the front of the house, past the head of the stairs, and saw Sheila's bedroom door an inch ajar. It closed as she watched.

She went into her own room, but not to sleep.

Chapter 24

CALLY STEPPED softly from her room into the corridor and glanced both ways along its length. She wore short, light cotton pyjamas and carried a soap bag, a prop in case anybody should look out and see her.

A line of brightness lit up the colours on a section of carpet to her left. It came from under Matt's door. The rest of the corridor was dark, except for the faint glow of the baseboard lights.

She stood for a moment, watching. The light from under Matt's door was a beacon that pulled at her. Suppose she turned the knob and walked in, would he welcome her? And if he did, would that be what she wanted?

All around, above and below, the old house sighed in its sleep. Downstairs in the parlour, the long-case clock struck three-quarters. Nearly midnight.

Cally turned and walked along the hallway, past the stairwell, to the door at the southeast corner, opposite Sheila's. She opened it, slipped inside, and closed it noiselessly. Then she turned on the light.

Aubrey lay sprawled on the bed, wide awake, wearing a pair of garish red boxer shorts patterned with images of Daffy Duck. He blinked at the light. "Darling! You've come for me at last!"

"Make room. We need to talk."

"Talk? What a waste!" But he sat up against the headboard and stuffed a pillow behind his back. Cally sat cross-legged at the foot of the bed.

"So your wheels have been turning too, eh?" he said.

"They've been turning for days, but especially since Ginny spilled the beans about being able to walk. I'm worried."

"So why aren't you in a huddle with Matt? Don't really trust him, right?"

She shook her head. "It isn't that. Aubrey, you and I are the only two outsiders. Even Mrs. Gardner is involved with the family. We're the only ones who can be objective."

"We can, can we? I wonder. Well, let's try." He pointed a long forefinger. "Starting with Matthew."

"Oh, have Sheila and Noel been filling your ears?" She uncrossed her legs, ready to jump off the bed. Then folded back down when she saw he was laughing at her.

"Objective!" He snorted.

"Well, how much of what you know is hearsay?"

"Some is." He shrugged against the headboard. "Some I got from Sheila, some from Ginny — yeah, she showed me that photo album. And some I figured out for myself."

"So you know Sheila and Noel are convinced Matt killed Gin's mother, and Jack Beamish as well. And Sheila suspects he has something to do with Vanessa disappearing. Did you also know that Noel hates Matt for stealing their father?" He opened his mouth; she held up a hand. "I'm convinced that's the way he sees it, and so it's the way Sheila sees it too. Neither one of them is capable of thinking about Matt in a rational way. They've made him a bogeyman — and I wouldn't put it past them to tell the police—"

"Hey! Easy! Easy, sweetheart!" Aubrey knelt forward and caught Cally's waving hands. She took a few deep breaths and pulled her hands free.

"Thanks. I'm okay. It's just — I know how easily Matt could be made to look bad. Especially with what happened to Jack."

"Well, he does seem to be the only person with a grudge against Jack — and good reason for it, too. And Noel kept refusing to fire the guy. Maybe that drove Matt too far."

"Hum. And why did Noel refuse to fire him? I know Jack was blackmailing somebody. Maybe it was Noel. Or maybe Sheila. That would give either of them a motive to push him off the cliff."

"Use your brains, Sheila would never—"

"Ha!" She stabbed a finger at him. "Who's being not objective now, eh?"

"Look," he said reasonably. "What could Jack possibly have on Sheila?"

"Don't know, but she's hiding something. She as good as told me so the other night. 'Things I did, things that could destroy me,' she said, but couldn't bear to tell me what."

"But I know her! You know her!" He waved both hands. "Seriously, what could she ever have done that's bad enough to need covering up?"

"Matt says folks around here suspect she pushed Francesca—"

"Crap!"

"Out of jealousy. Some of them suspect she did the same to Gin."

"Total horse shit!" He bounced off the bed and paced angrily.

"I agree with you there." She remembered Sheila's portrait of Ginevra: how lovingly the flowers surrounded and shielded the radiant girl. Sheila loved Gin, but had never been able to share her deepest feelings. Her demonstrations of affection either came across as stern and interfering, or they flew over Ginevra's head. "Which makes me wonder why she was following Gin this evening."

Aubrey dropped back onto the bed. "As if she was afraid for Gin. Afraid she might have seen or heard more than she lets on."

"Matt's worried too. He told me to keep an eye out."

"On the other hand, he could just be putting up a clever smoke screen."

Cally tossed up her hands. "What for? He knew two days ago that Gin's been mobile — and snooping. If he meant her any harm, surely—"

"But Gin's snooping didn't become a problem, if it has, until Jack was killed." He smiled smugly. "See, you can argue it any way you like."

"But Gin's not afraid of Matt. She's totally on his side. So she can't know anything bad about him, can she?"

"Oh no? We both know she'd lie her head off for him, no matter what he did."

Cally clutched at her hair. "If only I'd heard more of what Jack said, that time on the cliff!"

"Well, what did he say, exactly? Didn't he name anybody?"

"No. He didn't even say he or she." She closed her eyes tight and tried to think back. "He said something about how he had something — some information, I thought. How he'd been using it. And he said something about some female. What was it?" She opened her eyes. "'Piece of work, that girl.' That's what he said. Then he laughed." She twitched a shoulder in revulsion. "And then he said: 'Guess she got what was coming to her.'"

The silence stretched out. Aubrey sat with his arms around his bony knees and chewed his lip thoughtfully. Finally he said: "Who? Gin? Vanessa? Francesca?"

Cally got off the bed and went to the open window, hoping for a breeze. The air outside hardly stirred. The trees hung dead still. The darkness was total, the stars veiled. A thought struck her. She turned from the window.

"You can't see the cliff end of the island from here, can you?"

169

"No." Aubrey eyed her narrowly.

"So you never saw the lights in the cottage. Did you ever wonder if the vandalism, and the so-called ghostly lights, and the accidents — they might've all been meant to delay the work Matt's doing? Maybe even stop it?"

"Why would anybody want to do that?"

"I don't know. It just seems to me that an awful lot of mayhem centres on that cottage. Not just the vandalism, and not just those horrible old stories. There's Gin who fell near there, and Francesca too, and Jack. And as far as we can make out, the last place Vanessa was seen was up at the cottage."

"Where she met Matt, you mean." Aubrey nodded.

"Don't start that again!" She sank back onto the bed and rubbed her arms. "This is driving me crazy. If only we could clear it up once and for all!"

"Yeah, but how?"

They crouched in silence on the bed, facing each other. While Aubrey sat with eyes closed, apparently pondering, Cally's mind ran on to different things. She remembered other times they'd been together: the loving times and the painful, angry times. Yet looking at him now she felt only an uncomplicated fondness, as if the best of what they had been together remained after all the mistakes and betrayals had faded away.

"True friend, inconstant lover." She smiled at him.

"What?" He opened his eyes. "Still on about that? That's ancient history now, Cally. You no longer have a say."

"You ought to have Buyer Beware tattooed on your forehead."

"Why?" He spread his hands, all innocence. "I've always been honest about things. I never meant to deceive. All it takes is a good woman to keep me in line."

170

"Like Sheila?"

"Let's not get into that." His voice went flat. "You don't need to worry about her getting hurt, Cally. It's the other way round."

"So you really are serious? That would be a first."

"Yes, I'm serious!" he flared. Then collapsed inward, shoulders rounded. "She has this, this thing around herself, like a force field. I can't get close. I thought I could — she seems to like having me around — but holding hands is about as close as it gets."

"She has trouble with closeness. I think because she's afraid."

"Afraid of me?" He looked offended.

Cally shook her head. "Not you. I don't know what. Maybe everything. But you're right, she does like having you around. So hang in there. Be there for when she really needs you."

"Mm." Aubrey grimaced. "And that'll be when?"

"I think it might be soon."

"Huh." He gave her a measuring look. Then got off the bed and pulled a pair of jeans off the back of a chair. "Got your second wind?"

"For what?"

"What else have we been talking about? The cottage, right?"

"Well, yeah. The cottage."

"Worth a look, then."

"What, now?"

"What better time? Nobody else up and about." He bent to pull a pair of sneakers from under the bed.

"All right!" She slid off the bed. "Give me five minutes and meet me at the bottom of the back stairs."

Chapter 25

CALLY PULLED ON dark jeans, a black T-shirt and a pair of grubby old sneakers. She found a red bandana to cover her hair, and a small flashlight. When she stepped out into the corridor, feeling like a commando on a mission, all the other doors were closed. The house was silent, each member of the family shut into his or her private cell. She went quietly down the back stairs and found Aubrey at the bottom.

They left the house by the kitchen door, taking care not to let it slam, and trotted across the lawn in silence. The night was so dark that nobody would be likely to see them, Cally reasoned, even if anyone should be up and looking out a window at this hour. All the same, her shoulders stayed tight until they reached the woods.

Aubrey took the flashlight and went ahead along the path. He switched it on as they passed through the densest part of the woods. The light scared small hopping and flying things away on all sides, while attracting mosquitoes and big, bumbling moths. Cally made him switch it off.

In the clearings, their dark-adjusted eyes saw well enough to let them walk freely. The moon had grown a little. The thick, magnifying atmosphere turned it into a big, yellow, misshapen nail paring. It was the first time Cally had ever thought the moon ugly.

In the excitement of the excursion, she had forgotten how forbidding the cottage looked, especially by night. When they came within sight of it, she stopped short. Its squat shape, black against the veiled sky, was more than ever like a tomb. Or a barrow, a burial place so ancient it had become part of the rock and soil. And how many deaths had it seen?

"Come on," Aubrey said. "We don't have all night."

"Don't rush me, I don't want to sprain something."

Her steps lagged as they reached the house and rounded the corner. The place where Jack had gone over the cliff was only a few strides away. From somewhere in her mind's underworld crept an image of Jack standing on the cliff edge, drunkenly unaware, while the toadlike shape behind him stirred awake and opened its slitted eyes.

"Hey!" Aubrey grabbed her arm. She'd been inching backward. "Not scared, are you?"

"Scared? Of course not!"

Gulping down terror, she darted to the cottage door and snatched it open. Matt hadn't yet replaced the padlock. Aubrey stepped in behind her and swung the flashlight around. Her heartbeat steadied. There, that was better. Nothing here but lifeless wood and stone.

"Keep the light away from the windows," she said. "We don't want anyone to come investigating."

"Okay. Now what?" Aubrey moved the circle of light across the dusty floorboards, into the corners where Matt had arranged his tools and supplies, and up the makeshift supports to the hacked roof beam. "No attic to worry about. That simplifies things a bit. Maybe there's a hidey-hole behind these planks." He walked along the walls knocking on the wooden panels, listening for hollow sounds.

"Fireplace?" Cally peered into it, craned her neck to see up the flue, tapped unhopefully on the rough stones of its face.

"Aha! Here's a loose board!" Aubrey turned, grinning triumphantly. He tugged at one of the panels and it popped free into his hands. The flashlight went flying, sending its beam arcing crazily all over the room. Cally lunged and caught it before it could smash and leave them in the dark.

Then she poked the beam into the space behind the panel. "Looks like ... ugh." She reached in and pulled out something matted and mouldy-looking. "Old straw? Grass?"

"Insulation," Aubrey said, disappointed. "Guess you'd need that in the winters up here. Terrible fire hazard, though."

"Mm, yes. Matt will need to replace that."

Aubrey pushed the board back into place. Cally scrubbed her hand on her jeans and turned on the spot, looking all around. "So much for the great expedition. There's nothing here." The cottage was just an oblong box with no extra rooms, nothing built in, no niches, no secrets.

"There's really only one place where anything could be hidden." Aubrey tapped his sneaker toe on the floor. "The cellar."

Cally looked down at the floor without enthusiasm. "Matt said it's only about two feet deep, though. That's very shallow." *A shallow grave.* She wished she hadn't thought that.

She had always had a deep dislike and distrust of small, dark, earthy places. The cellar was always her least favourite part of any house. She wanted less than anything to go down there. But with Aubrey arching an ironic eyebrow at her, no way she was going to back out.

"Two feet is deep enough to hide lots of things." He held out a hand to the door. "After you!"

"Where? Oh, right." She'd forgotten about the little door outside that led to the cellar.

She walked out the door — and straight into something big and solid. She cried out and struggled wildly, only dimly aware of Aubrey's voice. Then the pressure relaxed, and she found herself leaning inside the warm curve of an arm, looking up.

"You!" he said.

"What d'you think you're doing?" Aubrey demanded. "Let her go!"

Matt removed his arms and stuck his hands in his pockets. The vague moonlight modelled his face into harsh planes. "What am I doing? I saw you two sneaking out, secretive as a pair of cats, so I followed. And what are you doing in my house?"

There followed an awkward pause, during which Aubrey, judging by the play of expressions across his face, invented and discarded a series of explanations. Matt's face grew steadily stonier. Cally wondered what, exactly, he had seen. Had he watched her go into Aubrey's room? She felt sick. Then furious.

"We're not here to sabotage anything!" she snapped. "We're guessing that the vandalism and the lights and so on were all to delay the work on the cottage."

"Why?"

"So that anything ... well, anything hidden here, wouldn't be discovered."

"And what could possibly be hidden here?"

"Who knows?" Aubrey broke in. "Are you going to let us search the cellar? Or are you going to stop us? You know how bad that would look."

"Has it entered your tiny brain," Matt said with ominous sweetness, "that the object of all that mayhem might have been to *attract* attention to the cottage? To create the impression that there is something here to be found?"

"To create suspicion around you, you mean?" Cally tried to puzzle this through. Then gave herself a shake. "Why don't we settle this once and for all? Matt, let us search the cellar. Please."

He was silent, his face in shadow, his features unreadable.

Aubrey gave a sudden whoop. "Hey! Now I know what's eating you! You saw Cally go into my room, didn't you?" A grin spread over his face. "And gosh, she was there a good half-hour. Long enough! And you're miffed because—"

"Don't be stupid!" Matt raised his head. Cally had been steeling herself for contempt, disgust, anger. She didn't expect a smile. He shot her a glance that caught the moonlight, an amused flicker. "You think I don't know Cally better than that by now?"

"Um. Yes?" Aubrey was taken aback.

"Yeah." He stabbed a finger. "So you watch how you talk about her, pal!"

Cally kept on an expression of offended dignity, the better to hide the warm place inside that made her want to smile.

"Oh. For sure." Aubrey took a deep, expansive breath. "So. The cellar?"

"Okay." Matt brought out the key (a detail Cally had forgotten), one of three on a ring from his pocket. They walked around the corner of the building to the cellar door. He unlocked the padlock and pulled it off, then threw back the door against the wall of the house.

A short flight of stone steps led down into blackness. The beam of Cally's flashlight, angled down to scan the floor, showed nothing but rough, bare rock and dirt.

"Can't see from here," Matt said. "We'll have to go in."

"I'll go first." Aubrey stepped down into the tiny doorway, sat on the top step, and slid himself in feet first. "Whoah!" he called back up. "Cobwebs!"

Cobwebs meant spiders. Cally was glad she'd thought to wear a scarf.

But there could be worse things than spiders.

Before her nerve could give way she stepped down into the stairwell, crouched, and slid in after Aubrey. "The floor's cold," she said, surprised.

"It's bedrock," Matt said. "The bones of the planet." He eased himself in last.

Aubrey took the flashlight and swept the beam into every corner. Nothing was there but themselves and their sliding shadows. It was just an empty, dusty, square box, floored and walled in rough stone.

Cally watched the beam slide over the low walls. "Funny — the shape is wrong. It's square. Shouldn't it be more long?"

"It is. That's a supporting wall, there." Matt pointed past Aubrey. "It runs across the centre, front to back. What we see here is only half the cellar. The other half is on the other side of that wall."

"Probably looks exactly the same." Aubrey ran the beam along the support wall.

"Wait!" Cally touched his arm. "What's that in the middle?"

The light ran back to the centre. Here was a difference in the pattern of the fieldstones. Cally crawled closer and brushed off some of the dust. "There's wood here. A square thing like a window frame."

"It's a hatch," Matt said. "Lets you go from one half the cellar to the other half, if you want. Or it used to."

"There are smaller stones inside the wood frame. I wonder who filled it in, and why?"

"No idea. It's been blocked off for as long as I can remember."

"Oh, good. That means we don't need to bother with it. We can get out of here." She glanced back longingly at the faintly glowing shape of the doorway.

"Right." Matt reached past her and brushed off more of the dust. A fleck of white appeared. His hand checked. "Now, that's funny."

"What?"

He fumbled in a pocket, brought out a folding knife, opened it and used the blade to scrape away some of the grit between the stones. Streaks of white showed bright in the flashlight beam. "Plaster," Matt said, in an odd, meditative voice.

"Shouldn't it be?"

"This support wall is like all the other walls. The stones are mortared. Or they were."

"So," Aubrey said, "whoever filled in this gate didn't know that, or thought it didn't matter."

"Matt." Cally was starting to get a glimmer. "You said it's been blocked off—"

"As long as I can remember." He turned on his side, propped on one elbow, to face her, but his face was invisible in shadow. "I remember coming down here when I was a kid. Maybe twelve. I found that wall and that filled-in hatch and of course I wanted to get through there, find out what was on the other side. I was sure there had to be something."

"Of course. So you broke it down?"

"Nope." His head moved in a negative. "That hatch was filled with stones that were *mortared* in, I'd swear to it. I was scared if I broke it, I'd bring the house down on top of me. Which wouldn't have happened, but at twelve I wasn't to know that. So, I backed out of there, went back in the house and pried up a couple of floorboards on the far side. And looked in. And guess what I found underneath?"

"What?" Cally breathed.

"Not a thing."

"Oh! But now there's plaster here, not mortar."

"That's right."

A beat of silence. Then Aubrey said: "You got a pickaxe?"

Matt crawled to the exit, which from the inside made a disturbingly tiny grey rectangle in the surrounding blackness. Cally followed him out. She sat at the top of the steps and pulled in deep lungfuls of the warm air, so thick and yet so fresh and clean after the cellar's dusty chill. The barely stirring breeze brought scents of lake water, dry grass and pine resin.

Too soon, Matt was back with a short-handled pickaxe and a hand-held floodlight. He slid down into the cellar again. Cally followed. He crawled to the centre wall and began hacking at the blocked gate. Leaning on his left elbow while wielding the pick with his right hand, he made a hole slightly larger than his head. Then he eased back. "Get some light in there."

Aubrey, who had taken charge of the floodlight, crawled forward and poked the powerful beam through the hole. He twisted his head this way and that. "Hard to see. I don't think—"

The light stilled. His breath hissed in. He reared back, bumping his head on a rafter. "Ow! Knock it all down."

Matt attacked the gate. Stones and plaster flew. Dust spread in choking clouds. Cally pulled off her scarf and covered her mouth and nose.

When the worst of the dust had settled, the light showed a square hole big enough that they could all see through to the other side. The cellar's second half was almost identical to the first half.

There was one difference. The second half held a long-term tenant. The bones were a patchy yellow-brown. They looked ancient, something that might have been dug up at an archaeological site.

"So this is what it was all about," Matt said in a flat, dead voice.

"Oh God," Aubrey said, and the beam wobbled. "Who was it?"

"Can't you guess?" Cally's voice shook. "Vanessa. She never left the island."

179

"And that's why." The beam focused unsteadily on what had been the head: pale rags of hair, dark eye sockets and a naked grin. And the crown of the skull was shattered like a glass bottle.

Chapter 26

THEY AGREED it would be best not to touch the bones.

"First thing tomorrow, I'll tell the police." Matt locked the cellar lid and slipped the key ring into his jeans pocket. "Until then, we keep it to ourselves. Best not to get anybody stirred up."

Cally wondered who he thought might get stirred up. And stirred up to do what? She would have asked him if he hadn't looked so flinty.

He circled back to the cottage door to put away the pickaxe and the floodlight, then returned. The moon was lower in the sky, the night was darker, but they switched on no light.

They were almost at the halfway point between the upper and lower ends of the forest path when Matt, barely visible a few steps ahead, stopped short. Aubrey bumped into him. "What—"

"Quiet!"

They stood frozen, listening. For ten thudding heartbeats, the only sounds were cricket song and the murmur of waves on the shore. Then, in the woods to their left, something moved with a crackling sound: something bigger than a raccoon or a fox.

"Who's there?" Matt called. No answer. "Is that you, Ginny?" Nothing. "Come on, you won't get in trouble. Ginny?" Nothing. Matt listened a moment longer, then lifted his head and said in a new, hard voice: "All right, I'm coming after you."

He took the flashlight from Cally's hand, switched it on and stepped off the path into the woods. Something crashed away from the light, eastward. Cally caught a glimpse of movement, enough to prove the lurker was human, but nothing else.

Matt swore, dashed back to the path, and raced toward the house. A few strides short of where the path opened onto the lawn he yelled and the light went spinning into the woods. Cally found him sitting on the path, nursing his right knee.

She knelt beside him. "What happened? Are you hurt?"

"Wrenched my knee. Nothing serious. That," he nodded downward, "wasn't there when we came out this way, was it?"

Aubrey had retrieved the still-lit flashlight from a patch of scrub. He shone it down. "That" was a thick branch lying across the path, skewed and splintered where Matt had tripped over it.

"Which tells me our lurker wasn't Ginny. This was too mean. Also too organized." He got to his feet, testing his knee gingerly. "This was done by somebody who planned ahead. They knew there was the chance of being spotted and chased, and they figured on a simple way to delay us long enough to get away."

"Somebody," Cally said slowly.

Aubrey pointed the flash down the path, looking for more traps. "Not a big field of suspects, is it?"

"No. But nothing I can prove." Matt limped on down the path.

Cally tried to remember exactly what they'd said aloud after locking the cellar. "Do you think they, whoever," she hesitated, "did they hear? Do they know what we found?"

"I think they already knew what was there," Matt said.

The house was dark when they crossed the lawn, and silent when they filed in the kitchen door. Matt, in the lead, moved quietly but made no effort to be soundless as he climbed the back stairs and walked along the corridor. He passed his own room and stopped at Ginevra's door, opened it, put his head in and listened. Pulled his head out and closed the door. Looked at Cally, smiled, murmured:

182

"Sound asleep."

He walked back to his own room, went in and closed the door.

Three people's footsteps, Cally thought, as she closed her own door. A voice. Three latches clicking home. Yet the rest of the house seemed sunk in an enchanted sleep. Even when she went to the washroom and scoured the cellar's dust and cobwebs from her hands and face, nothing and nobody stirred.

SHE WENT TO BED bone-tired and keyed up. She lay awake another hour. Each time she closed her eyes, images of a shattered skull surfaced from the dark behind her eyelids. The room seemed smaller than it should have been, the walls closer. She drifted into a doze from which she woke with a gasp, her hands pushing against the dark as if against wood nailed close above her face.

By rights she should have slept until noon, but anxiety goaded her awake at seven. Her room was already warm, the air seeping through the open windows like tepid bath water. Haze lay over the lawn and veiled the woods and the watery distance. She washed, dressed in shorts and a tank top and her old sneakers, and went downstairs to the breakfast room.

Noel and Ginevra were there. Noel, fresh from the shower and immaculate in short-sleeved white shirt and belted tan chinos, was placidly munching scrambled eggs and toast. Ginevra, in cut-off jeans and T-shirt, was digging into a big bowl of cereal heaped with strawberries and banana slices. "Sleep well?" Cally asked generally.

"Super," Gin mumbled through a mouthful.

"Pretty well, thanks." Noel smiled up at her. "And you?"

"Not really. Where's Sheila?"

"Still sleeping. I think she had a bad night. I heard her moving around in the small hours." He glanced up at the ceiling and grimaced. "The situation is really getting to her, poor kid. I wish the police would wind up this business of Jack and let us get on with our lives."

Wind it up how? By arresting Matt? She sat down with toast and coffee, but had to force herself to eat. She was standing at the sideboard pouring her third cup of coffee when there was a burst of footsteps in the hall. Then the front door banged. Through the window she saw Matt sprinting across the lawn to the woods.

"What was that?" Noel asked.

Cally turned to meet eyes: Noel's narrowly questioning, Gin's wide and excited. And Aubrey's, from where he stood unshaven and frowsy in the doorway, still in yesterday's clothes. He was blinking but alert and on edge.

"Just Matt going up to the cottage," she said.

"Ah." Noel returned to his breakfast. Aubrey crossed to the sideboard and muttered in Cally's ear, "The game is afoot."

"It's no game," she muttered back.

Sheila came down then, pale and silent. She stopped in the doorway, shot a look at Ginevra, then walked in and sat down. She was dressed, like Cally, for the heat, her dark hair twisted up. Cally almost heard the click as Aubrey's attention switched. He got busy pouring juice and asking Sheila what she would have to eat. She shook her head minimally. "Just coffee."

Cally leaned back against the sideboard, nursing her coffee and wishing it were iced. Her back was already prickling with sweat. Sheila gazed across the table at her in a musing way, as if she was weighing whether Cally should be told something, or asked something. Then she dropped her gaze to her hands.

They were all still there fifteen minutes later, when Matt came back and stood in the doorway, drawing all eyes the way a thunder-

184

cloud dominates a clear sky.

A moment of silence, while he scanned their faces. Then Ginevra sprang up crying, "Matt! What's wrong?" And Aubrey thumped down his coffee cup. "Don't tell me. The skeleton's gone."

"Skeleton!" Ginevra squeaked, and plumped back down.

Sheila said nothing, but seemed to shrink in on herself. Aubrey took her hand.

Noel said flatly: "I don't believe it."

"But Noel, there really is—" Cally began.

"I mean I don't believe the skeleton's gone. Not really." Noel's eyes stayed on Matt's. "I believe dear brother knows exactly where it is. Just as he's known all along."

"You're not surprised either," Aubrey commented.

Noel sent him a look of dislike. "Stay out of this. It's a family matter and it's complicated."

Matt took a step into the room. Cally caught his glance. "How did you know?" she asked.

"Got up this morning and the key ring was gone from my jeans." He smiled faintly. "I'm a heavy sleeper and everybody knows it."

"So anybody could have taken the key and moved the bones," Noel said thoughtfully. Then he smiled sweetly up at Matt. "Including you."

"Matt!" Ginevra sprang up again and hung on his arm, more like five years old than eleven. "What kind of bones? Are they, like a, a person's bones, or a dog's bones, or—"

"Gin," said Sheila flatly, "leave him alone."

Ginny ignored her. So did Matt. He freed his arm, put a knuckle under her chin and tilted her face up. Her eyes were dark with fright. "Not to worry, kidlet. I'll tell you all about it, but not right this minute."

"No fair! Nobody ever tells me *anything!*"

"Go on, now." He tapped the end of her nose. "Make like a bunny and hop it. Okay?"

She blinked up at him, then pulled away, her mouth trembling. "Oh, all *right!*" She flounced out of the room. Cally didn't think she'd ever seen anyone flounce before, but she was pretty sure Gin had nailed it. A minute later the slam of her bedroom door echoed through the house.

"Good that she stays out of the way," Noel said. He pushed back his chair and got up. "The obvious thing now is to tell the police."

"The obvious thing now is to find the bones." Matt gazed impassively at his brother. "The sooner the better. Who'll help me search?"

"I will," Cally said.

Noel held up a hand. "No, Cally, if you don't mind, I'd like you to stay with Sheila. This is knocking her sideways. I don't want her left alone."

Sheila straightened in her chair and muttered, "Ridiculous." But Cally saw what Noel meant. She was haggard and pale, her eyes ringed with sleepless purple. She looked ill.

"I'll stay with Sheila." Aubrey reached for her again but she shook his hand off.

"You go away," she said. "I'll be fine."

"Go away? Where?"

"Anywhere." Not looking at him she added, "I don't want you here."

Aubrey went white. In a moment he pulled back the breath that had been knocked out of him, got up and headed for the door. As he passed, Matt gripped his shoulder and swung him around. "Hey. You helped spill this can of worms, you'd better help clean it up."

Cally was afraid Aubrey might take a swing at him, but after a

186

heartbeat his hands relaxed. He nodded and went out. Matt followed him. Cally went with them as far as the front door and watched them cross the lawn and vanish up the forest path. She blinked against the glare of the haze-scattered sunshine and wiped a trickle of sweat from her neck.

"You will stay with Sheila?" Noel asked, suddenly behind her.

"Of course, if she wants me."

"Even if she doesn't. Cally, I'm worried about her. I wish I could be in two places at once!"

"You're going to the police, then?"

"Yes. It's about time."

"Noel." She turned and met his eyes, very blue in the morning light. "How long have you known about this? It's Vanessa, isn't it?"

"I believe so. I never knew for sure, but I always suspected something like this." He blinked and looked away. "Please, just do this thing for me. Stay with Sheila. She needs you. I'll be back as soon as I can."

Chapter 27

CALLY WENT BACK to the breakfast room to clean up, but found the table and sideboard already cleared. She went on into the kitchen. "Can I help with the washing up?"

"Thank you kindly, but no." Mrs. Gardner looked grim. "Best you stay with Sheila. She'll be needing you soon enough." She hesitated, then added, "I'll be leaving as soon as I've finished here."

"Leaving?"

"For good. I'm already packed. This island is no place for sane people — Jack killed and skeletons dug up and Lord knows what else— Well. If the police want me they can find me at home in Blackwater Bay." She turned her back, signalling End of Conversation.

Cally backtracked out of the kitchen. In the front hall she met Sheila coming down the stairs. "We don't need to worry about Gin for now," Sheila said. "I made her go into my room and lock the door on the inside."

"That's good. But who exactly are you afraid of?"

Sheila didn't answer. She drifted into the parlour and across to the piano, and began poking tunelessly at the keyboard. Cally thought: Piano = Aubrey.

"You weren't serious, were you?"

Sheila didn't look around. "About what?"

"Telling Aubrey you don't want him here. I know you like him."

Sheila ran a hand over the keys, pulling up a jangle of notes.

"And more than like."

"Cally, why bother?"

"Because he's good for you. And you're good for him, it seems to me. And it would be nice to salvage something from this wreck."

Sheila laughed helplessly, shaking her head. "You always were such an optimist."

"But why—"

"All right, I'll tell you. I was going to anyway." She straightened up like an old woman, stiff and slow. "Come on, let's walk."

THE LONG-CASE clock struck nine as they left the house. Only nine? To Cally it felt hours later than that. They wandered slowly across the lawn and under the windless trees, then up through the woods toward the island's crest, picking their way, not taking any path. And all the while, Sheila talked.

"I'm not going to rake over our miserable childhood again," she said. "You already know most of it. How our father adopted Matt and loved him, and how after Noel and I were born, we were always the afterthought, Noel especially. And yes, we figured out that Matt was Dad's bastard, and we knew what the word meant. He was a walking insult. He was evidence that our father had not loved our mother, or not enough.

"Then Mother died. And Noel always felt that somehow Matt helped cause her death. Not by anything he did, just by the fact that he existed. Seeing him every day must have eaten at her just as the cancer did. Irrational, yes, but that's what Noel felt.

"Later, Dad pressured Matt to join the carpet import business, and Matt just flat refused. Said he wanted to be an architect." Sheila waved her hands. "What a dust that raised! Months of shouting! Dad refused to finance Matt's studies. Matt refused to compromise. He worked his way through the co-op program at Waterloo. Said he

189

wouldn't take a nickel from Dad even if it were offered."

"Well, that's good, right?"

"Oh, yes." Sheila smiled thinly. "Dad certainly thought so. Matt flouted him and went his own way, and Dad *respected* that. He never said so, but you could see it all over him, the pride. Meanwhile Noel had announced that he planned to study business management and go into the family business. He did everything he could to live up to Dad's expectations. He tried to be the perfect son. And Dad, I think, hardly noticed.

"And then there was Francesca. An intruder like Matt, another slap at Mother's memory. You know what happened to her, and what we think about that. But then there was Gin." Sheila's voice softened. "She was just five when her mother died. That was the year we started at TCU, remember? I went home to Ginny as often as I could. I tried to be a mother to her. I taught her how to tell time, how to count. I bought her clothes. She showed me all her little projects from school." A smile warmed her face.

"I was the one who spotted her musical ability and got her started with lessons. I loved her. And I tried, I tried so hard to be a mother to her. But she never loved me. Matt, though: she loves him. He never did a thing for her, and she loves him. How fair is that?"

They came out of the woods into the heavy sunshine of a clearing on the crest of the island. Some long-ago lightning strike had burned away the forest here. Much of it had grown back, but the centre still held a few square yards of yellowing witch grass, buttercups, thistles and wild carrot. The dry, aromatic smell that rose from under their feet made Cally think of camomile tea.

"Let's rest," she said. What would have been a pleasant stroll last week was exhausting in this steamy heat. Her sleeveless top stuck to her back, and her head was aching. She sat down on the grass in the patch of shade under the trees, stretching her bare legs out in front.

Sheila stayed standing. Cally squinted up at her, wishing she would sit down, and wondering if Matt and Aubrey were anywhere near.

Dark tendrils suddenly fanned out around Sheila's head. A breeze had sprung up. Cally looked past her into the distance. From this height, looking northwest, the view stretched for miles and miles. You could see half of the long island-studded lake, and beyond that all the way to the horizon, where a range of purple hills cut scallops out of the haze-whitened sky.

She pointed. "What are those hills?" And almost in the same moment recalled that there were no hills in that direction. That was where the land began its slope toward Georgian Bay.

"They're not hills, they're clouds," Sheila said.

"Oh thank God, the rain's coming!"

"And it's going to be a soaker." Sheila sank down onto the grass beside Cally. "I'd better wrap this up before the weather catches us," she said in a brisk, everyday voice. "Here's what I really wanted to tell you, the thing that explains everything that's been happening around here lately. Vanessa."

"Those bones."

"Yes. Her bones. I know because I put her in that cellar."

Cally held her breath and only let it out when her heart began banging in her ears. "You?"

Sheila picked at the dry grass and watched the distant clouds. "Yes, me. I had to, for Dad's sake. I guess I did a pretty good job, too." She laughed. "Because the police hardly looked into it. I wrote a note — I have a talent for forgery, it seems — telling Noel she was leaving, and not to follow her. He never knew about it, by the way; but I think he suspected. That's why he wasn't surprised this morn-

191

ing."

"He never knew? But, Sheila, what are you saying? Are you trying to tell me you killed Vanessa?"

"Let me finish. I put her in the cellar — which was damned hard, let me tell you — and then I blocked up that gap. Then I took her suitcases, with all her clothes in them, and before anybody else was up I took one of the boats to Port Devon, and rented a car using her ID and credit card. I'd covered my hair and wore dark glasses, and anyway the clerk was new. That was a lucky break. Then I drove to Toronto and took a plane to New York. The night before, I'd told Dad and the others that I wanted to be left alone in my rooms for the day, to work. It seems nobody wondered or cared about that, except Noel. But he never asked any questions. I got rid of the suitcases and flew back. Reappeared late that day. There: done and dusted!

"And then I think I went a little mad."

"Oh, Sheila. If you'd told me—"

"You couldn't have helped. Not in any way. I couldn't stop picturing how she looked with her head caved in. It took a while for me to get back to normal — or as near normal as was possible for me." Sheila laughed again. Then she sighed. "This next part is harder. Jack saw some of what happened with Vanessa and got hold of the wrong end of the stick, typically. He thought it was me who killed her and he started blackmailing me."

"Oh!" Cally threw up her hands. "Of course it wasn't you! For a while there you really had me going!"

"Yeah. At first he was modest about it. He usually disguised the demand as a request to be repaid for doing extra jobs or carrying out errands in the village while the family were in Toronto. After Dad died, though, he got bolder. I think he assumed I was rich now, or I could get money from Noel, so I could afford to pay."

"And his leverage? I see." Cally rubbed her aching forehead. "You didn't kill anybody, but you covered up a crime. The truth won't hurt your father now, but it'll hurt you."

"Yes. I looked it up. If I'm arrested and convicted it could mean years in prison. I don't think I'd survive in one of those places." She drew a breath. "That's why I killed him."

"Wait — Sheila—"

"I killed Jack," she said firmly, as if Cally was disputing it. "I pushed him off the cliff. Because he wouldn't leave me alone. He threatened to tell the police, he said he'd tell everybody. I couldn't let that happen. So, yes, I killed Jack. And that's why Aubrey has to go away, because I don't want him near me once he knows. I don't want to see his face when he finds out what I've done."

Chapter 28

SOMEONE WAS WALKING through the trees to the east: walking quietly, but not trying to be silent. Cally thought wildly of a hunting animal, a big cat, and instantly discarded the notion. But fear was in the air. She stood up and Sheila did too, and instinctively they drew closer together.

Then Noel pushed through a curtain of sumacs into the clearing, and Sheila laughed with relief.

"Hello, you two." His thin, anxious face lit up with a smile. "Thought I heard voices. What brings you up here on such a morning?" He looked at the slowly rising purple in the west. Then his eyes fixed on something in the woods on the far side of the clearing.

Branches crackled, and Matt stepped into the open. Aubrey crunched out after him, batting away flying bugs. He stopped short when he saw Sheila but Matt came on, relaxed, at a saunter.

Noel smiled. "Well, this is opportune, all of us being here. I'm just back from OPP Port Devon. They say they're chronically under-staffed and overworked, and now it's worse than ever, with Jack's case on their hands. They're too busy to come and look for misplaced bones at a moment's notice." He flicked a razor glance at Matt.

"So when will they come?" Matt inquired.

"Noon at the earliest. Later, if the storm hits first."

Everyone looked to the west. The band of purple hills looked like mountains now. They swelled even as Cally watched. "We should get back to the house," she said.

"Yes, we should." Noel held out a hand to Sheila, who clasped it.

"In any case the police want us all to stay indoors as much as possible. And they don't want anybody interfering with the remains until they get here."

"Why don't you just say where you stashed them?" Matt said easily. "Save the cops some trouble."

"Let's cut the charade, all right? And one more thing." Noel lifted his head. His eyes were blue lights aimed at Matt. "Ginevra. I've been looking all over for her. Where is she?"

"Gin?" Matt stuck his hands in his pockets. "How would I know?"

"Oh, you would." Noel dropped Sheila's hand and took a hard step toward Matt. "What have you done with her?"

"Don't be an ass." Matt's eyes were blank silver coins in this light.

Sheila gripped Noel's arm and pulled him away. "Come on, let's get back. You can't have looked everywhere. For Gin, I mean. Did you look in my room?"

"No, but I called and she never answered. And she's not on the beach."

"I put her in my room. She's keeping her head down. She's fine." She started him across the scrubby meadow, eastward. "And about the bones. Noel, it's all right. You don't have to keep pretending for my sake."

"Sheila—" He stopped and pulled away to get a look at her face.

"I said it's all right!" She laughed, lighthearted. As if a mountain of dread had suddenly lifted from her shoulders. "Of course you moved them. You saw them being found, last night, and you were trying to protect me, as always. But you don't have to any more. I've told Cally everything."

"My God, Sheila—"

195

"Yes, the whole thing. How after he murdered Vanessa," she tilted her head at Matt, "I covered it up to protect Dad. Because it would've hurt Dad too much."

"Wait!" Cally started after them. "How Matt— How would you know?"

Sheila ignored her and everybody else, speaking only to Noel. "How you knew nothing about it — so don't try to shoulder the blame now! How Jack was blackmailing me, and I killed him because it couldn't go on. He would have ruined us."

"Sheila, no—" He seized both her hands.

"Just listen! The old fool thought it was me who'd killed her. But now the skeleton is out of the closet!" She flashed a slightly manic grin. "So I'll have to tell the police, won't I?" She looked at Cally and quickly away. "I'll have to tell them everything I know. Everything."

Aubrey suddenly bounded forward. "I don't believe a word of it! Cally, you can't let her do this!"

Sheila gave him an icy look. "You were hired as a piano teacher. Nothing else. Why don't you keep your nose out of what's none of your business?" Aubrey turned his back, but not before Cally had seen the grimace of pain on his face.

Noel and Sheila walked away into the woods arm in arm. Matt watched them go. He looked, Cally thought, like a man pondering a move in chess. Or in war.

He looked at her and a smile warmed his eyes. "So, we're in for some weather. I guess we'd better get back."

"I guess so." She shook her head, which was buzzing with shocked questions. "Does that mean you're going to sit quietly like a good boy and wait for the police?"

"What do you think?" He started across the clearing. Over his shoulder he said, "You may recall, or not, that I never got any breakfast. I need food and coffee. Then I'll search again before the storm breaks."

Cally tried sorting out her thoughts as they picked their way back toward the house. "Some of this stuff I just can't accept," she said. "I can see Sheila covering up a murder, for your father's sake. Although it would haunt her, and it has. But I can't seriously see her hitting out at Jack."

"It's total crap," Aubrey muttered behind them.

Matt said quietly, "I wish I knew what Noel's planning right now."

"He called in the police," Cally said. "He plans to get you charged with murder."

"He might try."

"Matt, what does Sheila know? What makes her so sure?"

He smiled down at her, and away. "Remember what I said about something bad coming? I think it's almost here. And I want you to stay out of it. Will you promise me that?"

"Will you be involved in it?"

"Of course."

"Then no, I can't stay out of it." She laughed, not merrily. "Anyway it's too late. I'm in it up to my eyeballs!"

"Cally, haven't you noticed? Things happen around me. Nasty things. I'm not asking, I'm telling you. Stay the hell away from me!"

He strode on. She kept up, but the conversation was over.

Chapter 29

IT WAS TEN-THIRTY when they got back to the house. Noel was standing in the front hall looking up the stairs. "Sheila's gone up to liberate Gin," he said.

Aubrey stalked past him as if he wasn't there, went into the parlour and slammed the door. Matt went to the kitchen. He came out again a moment later, handed Noel a folded paper, and went back in.

"It's from Mrs. Gardner." Noel stood in the light of the front doorway, scanning the note. "She's quit. Packed up and gone. She's taken the outboard and I'll find it at the wharf in Blackwater Bay." He folded the note and put it in his shirt pocket. "Can't blame her, I suppose. We'll just have to fend for ourselves until we can leave."

Sheila came running down the stairs. "She's not there! She's gone!"

"Take it easy!" Noel held out his hands to her but she brushed them away.

"I need to know where she is!"

"She could be anywhere, couldn't she?" Cally said. "Roaming about, as usual." But worry prickled up her spine.

"No, she can't have gone far, not with a storm blowing up. She's scared of lightning. I'll check the cellar."

"She's scared of lightning?" Noel looked surprised.

"You didn't know that?" She gave him a reproachful look, then clattered down the cellar stairs.

A breeze swirled in, surprisingly cool. Noel's fine hair blew upward. He brushed it down, turned and looked out across the lawn. "I wonder if there's time," he said, as if to himself. Cally looked past him. The stretch of the lake that was visible through the trees was a dull pewter grey, all glitter gone. White crests edged the waves.

Into the stillness of the hall came a long eerie whistle that raised the hairs on the back of Cally's neck. She opened the parlour door. It was wind: a rising west wind that poured through the screened windows. The long, heavy drapes were billowing out like flags.

Aubrey was sitting at the piano, staring at the keys, hands limp in his lap. "Aubrey—"

"Leave me alone."

She left him alone and crossed the room to close the windows. Then she went through the other rooms on the ground floor, closing all the windows, battening down for the storm. Noel stood watching, then nodded brightly, as if inspired. "I'll do the second floor." He sprang up the stairs. Thuds and bangs followed.

He was coming back down when Sheila came up from the cellar. "Not there. I searched the whole place." She stood staring around the hall, as if hoping to find Gin hiding behind the furniture.

"Sheila, look." Noel held out his hand. A small medication bottle lay on his palm. "You're all tied up in knots. Go up and lie down, sweetheart, and take a couple of these."

"What's that?" Cally asked, from the parlour doorway.

"Her anti-anxiety meds. Go on up, Sheila. I'll get you some water to wash it down."

She shook her head violently. "I hate that stuff. It makes me dopey. We have to find Gin."

"The police will find Gin," Noel said patiently. "If they just question—"

He broke off. Matt came out of the kitchen brushing crumbs from his hands. "I'm off," he said.

"Where, to search for the bones? You know what the police said."

"I know what you said." Matt gave him a smiling look. He turned, his eyes sliding over Cally's as if she wasn't there. Through the door to the parlour he called, "Aubrey! You coming?"

Aubrey came out wordlessly, not looking at anyone.

"Right," Matt said briskly. "We've covered most of the northwest shoulder. We'll start on the south slope near the cottage."

Noel kept his eyes on them as they crossed the lawn to the forest path. He watched them out of sight, then stood a moment in thought, blinking at the doorframe. Then nodded decisively and swung around to look from Cally to Sheila. "I'm going straight back to Port Devon. See if I can hurry the police along. And they need to know we can't find Gin. On the way back I'll pick up the outboard from Blackwater Bay."

"But the storm," Sheila began.

"There should just be time if I go now." He glanced back out the open door, in the direction Matt and Aubrey had gone. "I'd feel a lot happier if you would lock yourselves in your rooms until I get back."

"For heaven's sake!" Cally didn't know whether to laugh or slap him.

"I'm serious. You think you know Matt, Cally, but you are so wrong. There are things you don't know and I hope you never have to find out." Something, either apprehension or memory, drained life and colour from his voice. Cally was chilled. Then, with a stride, he was gone.

"Well," Sheila said, "I'm going upstairs."

"What for, to lock yourself in? To dope yourself?"

"That sounded bitter!" Sheila paused with a hand on the newel post. "No and no. I'm still not convinced Noel did a really thorough search. Gin might still be in the house."

"But without a peep? She'd have to be hiding — from us — and why would she do that?"

"Spooked, probably. Enough's happened, these last few days, to scare any kid, let alone a fine-wired drama queen like Gin. The only place I haven't looked is the top floor."

"I'll go with you."

The third floor was so empty that their footsteps echoed. Only three bedrooms had been occupied, and now all the occupants had gone: Edna in a panic, Mrs. Gardner with grim decision, and Jack forever.

"I have to say I'm surprised at Mrs. Gardner," Cally said, looking around the housekeeper's spic-and-span deserted room. "I had the impression that nothing short of the Apocalypse would shake her loose."

"Same here." Sheila pulled her head out of the closet. "She's been with us even longer than Jack. Used to come here as a girl, with her grandmother, who was the housekeeper then. She — Mrs. G — was absolutely loyal to Dad. I think she was sweet on him." She smiled, then looked thoughtful. "She has a soft spot for Matt too, come to think of it."

Edna's room was equally bare and clean and empty. Jack's room was the exception. They stood together in the doorway gazing around. Sheila said: "Mrs. G never came in here with a duster, that's plain to see."

The room was an amalgam of bed-sitter, tool shed, entertainment hub and recycling depot. One wall lined with industrial shelving and pegboard held an impressive stock of hardware supplies and tools, all neatly arranged. Cartons of empty beer and liquor bottles were stacked in the corners. Another wall was dominated by a large television and several shelves of paperback westerns.

They called Gin's name but got no answer. Sheila knelt to look under the bed while Cally crossed to the closet. The door opened on more cartons of empties, so many that there was hardly room left for a handful of shirts on hangers. She backed out. "Uh-uhn. Gin isn't here. Is there an attic?"

"Yes, but it's unfinished — no floorboards," Sheila said absently. She was at the window, gazing out at Jack's magnificent view of the lake and woods. "Um, Cally, would you please check the closet again? Gin could have made a hollow for herself behind those boxes." She turned from the window and strode across the room to the doorway. "I'll have a look in the linen closet out here."

"Well, all right, but I don't think—" A metallic *snick* whirled her around. The door of the room was closed. She tried the knob. It sat solid. Cally rattled it and pounded on the door. "Sheila! What the hell? Sheila!"

Below, the front door slammed. Cally ran to the window and saw Sheila racing across the lawn toward the woods. She pushed open the window and yelled, but Sheila either didn't hear or didn't want to hear.

"Sheila!" Cally beat on the window frame with her fists. Sheila was out of sight now. Only one place she could be heading: the cliff end of the island. Where Matt and Aubrey were searching for Vanessa's bones.

But why go there? To confront Matt? Why now? To collar Aubrey, beg him to forget the cruel things she'd said? Why all of a sudden?

Cally was alone in the house now. Everybody else was gone. *Something's happening,* Matt had said. *Something's wrong.* Something very wrong. Wrong enough to knock all thoughts of Ginevra out of Sheila's head. And it was happening right now up at the cottage.

The cottage. That's where I have to be, not locked up here at the top of the house like some stupid princess in a tower!

But how to get out? The window? She opened it as wide as it would go and lifted out the screen. The window was big enough to climb out of, but too high to climb down from, and there were no handy trellises, downspouts or ledges. Jump? She looked out and down. Yes, and go splat on the terrace stones three storeys below.

She closed the window and turned around. There had to be a way. Ladder? Maybe Jack had one of those fold-up ladders in case of fire. She ran across to the hardware shelves. There were all kinds of tools here: hammers, saws, awls, chisels, screwdrivers in a spectrum of sizes and types. No ladder.

Screwdrivers, though....

Memory stirred. Herself at twelve locked into the basement, a place she feared and hated, with her three brothers chortling outside the door, waiting for her to scream and beg. They'd forgotten about the tools that were kept in the basement. And perhaps they'd never noticed that the door's hinges showed on the inside.

Cally went over to examine the door of Jack's room, then chose her tools.

Chapter 30

THE WIND ATTACKED her as she opened the front door. She had to pull hard on the handle to close it behind her. As she crossed the terrace a wave of torn leaves and flower heads lashed her legs. A flicker caught her eye. Tongues of lightning darted beyond the lake to the west. The storm was nearly on the doorstep.

She started across the lawn toward the forest path at a run, then skidded to a stop. *Think!* Sheila had gone that way, and in a big hurry. If she followed the same path, as soon as she was out from under the trees anyone in the cottage could look out of those slit windows and see her coming across the meadow. That might not be the best plan.

Better to come at the cottage from the south, where the woods crowded up the bluff to within a few yards of the building.

Down to the beach, then, and the empty pier. From there she ran westward, leaving the sand behind, clambering over boulders, pushing aside low branches and jerking free of wild grapevines. Once her ankle turned on a pile of pebbles. She staggered on, wincing. Dry bracken and raspberry canes rasped at her bare legs.

On the southwest curve of the island Cally sank down, panting, on a heap of shingle. The wind whipped her hair and iced the sweat on her neck. Overhead the clouds crowded thick and purple on the heels of the ochre sun. Next moment they buried it, sending a flood of shadow over land and water. The lake went from pewter to sullen black.

Something banged, not far away. Cally shot to her feet. That wasn't thunder. It sounded like a door slamming, or a stone falling on stone, hard, from a height. Or fireworks. Or....

Not a gun. Nobody here had a gun. Please God.

Get on! She scrambled over the boulders, which were larger now, wincing as her foot pressed down. Then pushed through a curtain of young trees and shrubs that grew down to the water. And found a surprise. A boat pulled up on the shingle, in among the shrubs where it wouldn't be seen from the lake. A good-sized red boat. Noel's boat.

So Noel hadn't gone to Port Devon after all. He'd circled back. And Sheila, from that third-floor window, had seen.

But why keep me out of it?

With that thought came, again, the sound like a slamming door. No doubt now. A second gunshot.

Westward the trees ended, except for a frill of brush at the base of the cliff. The cottage must be almost directly above where she stood now.

Cally threw herself at the cliff path and went up like a squirrel, clawing at the wiry cedars, her sneaker toes gouging the fibrous dirt. She nearly missed the place where the path divided. One branch snaked to the right around a stony outcrop and up the shrubby south-west curve of the bluff. Another branch led left, at first plain and easy going, out to the island's tip, ending above the stone face.

For a moment she clung to the outcrop and traced with her eyes how she'd missed this branching in the dark that other night, the time she'd climbed down from above and ended up on the boulder above the giant's brow ridge.

The giant's face: the perfect place to eavesdrop on anything going on in the cottage, with the cottage door only a couple of yards away.

It would also be the most dangerous place. Once you were

perched on that rock below the brink, anyone who walked near the edge could look down and see you. You'd be as helpless as a black spider on a white wall. Especially when the one above had a gun.

Cally breathed deeply a moment, then climbed on up the right-hand path. She scrambled out at the top and threw herself down behind a screen of drought-bitten sumacs and yellow bracken.

About four yards away the cottage squatted low and black against the streaming clouds. The slit windows seemed to squint at her malevolently. Stronger than ever, she sensed a presence inside, a spirit that wore those stones and timbers the way a hermit crab wears a shell. And it was aware of her.

For one despairing moment she could not, physically, force herself to go any nearer. Then voices came to her ears. They were in the cottage. She had to go there.

But they'll see me!

Not if I keep low. Maybe. Worth a gamble. Because staying here will do no good at all.

She pushed through the crackling stems on hands and knees. Then, still crawling, she crept across the meadow toward the cottage.

Chapter 31

NOBODY HAILED HER. When she reached the house she stood up and flattened herself against the stone wall next to one of the windows, close to the front corner. She eased her head around the corner to see the door. It looked to be open, so far as she could see from here. Nobody was visible in the doorway.

Her foot nudged a chunk of loose stone. It grated against the wall. She stood paralyzed, but still no challenge came.

"I really wish you hadn't come here," Noel said, so close and distinct that Cally thought he was talking to her. Before she could move or reply he added, "You must have been up on the third floor, is that how you saw me coming back?"

Sheila murmured something.

"Where's Cally, then?"

"Still there," Sheila said more loudly. "I locked her in."

"That's good. I want her kept out of this."

Cally breathed again. She edged back to the slit window, her face to the wall, and moved her head until she could see in. And almost cried out with relief. Matt was there, alive and well. He sat on the floor, his back against the opposite wall, knees bent up in front. He seemed to be leaning back on his arms. At least, his arms were behind him, and she couldn't see his hands.

Then, with a grimace, he straightened his left leg, and Cally saw the shining wet patch that reddened the denim on the outside of the thigh. *Oh God.*

"Keep still, you." Noel stood facing Matt, gun aimed and steady in his right hand, his left jingling the change in his trousers pocket. Barely suppressed glee tugged at the corners of his mouth. "The first shot was to get your attention. The second was to show you I'm serious. The third will finish you. So don't push me."

"Where'd you get the gun?" Matt said coolly. "I bet it's not registered."

"There are ways and means. I knew this day would come, so I made sure I was ready." Noel's voice was suddenly louder, and Cally tensed, until she realized he'd stepped into the doorway. "Still a couple of boats out on the lake," he said. "We need to wait until they're all gone. Won't be long." Thunder boomed distantly. The whole sky was purple now.

"Noel." Sheila's voice quivered. "You can't do this. I won't let you."

"Now, don't try to stop me." He sounded fond. "You're a dear and you mean well, but my mind's been made up a long, long time. Years. There's only one way this can finish."

Cally edged back to the window. Matt sat in the same position, only now it was obvious that his hands were fastened behind his back. Plenty of rope or wire in there to do the job. But Matt wouldn't stand still for that, and Noel couldn't have managed it while holding a gun on him. So how was it done?

"I can even tell you the exact date I began planning this." Noel waved his left hand. His right, with the gun, stayed rock-steady. "It was two days before my twelfth birthday. You remember, Matt?"

"Can't say I do."

"You and I were with Dad. He'd taken us to work with him. Sheila, you were home sick that day, or you'd remember this for sure. A man came into the office, a business acquaintance. Dad introduced us, his two sons. The man knew one of us was adopted, he didn't

208

know which. Said he could guess. Remember now?"

"Sorry, no." Matt's eyes never left Noel's face.

"Funny, to me it's like it happened yesterday. The guy picked me for the adopted son. Me. He said it was obvious who the chip off the old block was. That was you, Matt. Still don't recall?"

"No."

"Too bad. Because that was a special moment. I hoped we could remember it together. That was the moment I knew someday I would kill you."

Cally spotted Aubrey a little beyond Matt. He was lying on his side, wrists and ankles wrapped with what looked like duct tape. His eyes were closed, his mouth slack. Sheila knelt next to him, one hand on his shoulder and the other on his head.

She could almost see it happening. Noel finds Matt and Aubrey near the cottage, demonstrates that his gun works just fine, herds them inside. Matt lunges at Noel. Noel shoots him in the leg and orders Aubrey to tape his hands. Noel then knocks Aubrey out and tapes him. Sheila arrives at a run and doesn't get hit or taped up, because she's Noel's twin, his lifelong best friend, the one person who would do anything for him.

At that moment Sheila looked straight at Cally through the window. Cally jerked back out of sight. No point trying to run. She held her breath.... And let it out when Sheila said, "Noel, listen. People have died. Nobody else has to die. Not even Matt."

Noel laughed gently. "Well, there I'm afraid you're wrong."

"But think of the risk! The police aren't stupid. When two more bodies turn up, we'll be under the spotlight. They'll really start digging, and—"

"And you aren't all that strong, are you? Apt to cave in under pressure? Don't worry, dear, I've thought of that. Matt will take the blame for everything."

"How do you figure that?" Matt's voice. He sounded merely curious. Cally edged forward again so she could see.

"This is how it will go. In brief," Noel held up his left forefinger. "Matt will quarrel with Aubrey over Cally, and Matt — everyone knows what a temper he has — Matt will throw Aubrey off the cliff."

"No!" Sheila leaped to her feet.

"Sorry, but yes. Then, knowing he'll never cover this one up, Matt will go back into the cottage, write his confession, and blow his brains out with this very gun." His voice smiled. "Simple! Simple is best, don't you think?"

Do something! Cally railed at herself. *Stop this!*

But how? Walk in, startle Noel, grab the gun? Or climb back down the hill, take the boat and go for help? The first might be suicide, the second too late.

"Call me dense, but what makes you think I'll write a confession?" Matt asked, still apparently just curious.

"You won't write it, actually. Sheila will. We'll put those talents to use again, okay, Sheila? Have him confess to killing Francesca, Vanessa, Jack and Aubrey. That should do it. The bones won't matter then. And neither you nor I will know anything about anything."

"Noel." Sheila stepped forward, palms up. "Look. You don't need to kill Aubrey, he doesn't know any more than Cally."

"He does now. He's heard everything. He can't be allowed to go around blabbing." Noel gave Aubrey's knee a kick. "Yes, I know you're playing possum. You can stop faking."

Aubrey groaned and rolled over onto his back. Sheila looked down at him, then back at her brother. She was standing between him and his two prisoners. Cally wondered if she knew how dangerous that was, and if she was planning something stupid and heroic, like

210

going for his gun.

Got to move, do something. Distract him!

"If you kill him," Sheila said, "you might as well kill me too. I love him." Aubrey's eyes opened wide.

Noel laughed. "You aren't serious!"

"I am."

"Don't you know he's been jerking you around? Sheila, I saw Cally go into his room last night. Fact! She was in there a good half hour. What d'you imagine they were doing, chatting?"

Aubrey croaked, "That's exactly what we—"

"Shut up! Sheila, don't you see he's just after you for a meal ticket?"

"I don't believe that. I don't believe what you said about Cally, either. She's flat-out in love with Matt, the poor kid. She's convinced he's completely innocent."

"Cally? Don't be silly. She's attracted, obviously, and maybe infatuated, but she's too smart to fall for an animal like that. Anyway, once she's read his confession, she'll know what a lucky escape she's had."

His last word was buried in an avalanche of noise as lightning ripped open the sky above the lake. As the last crash died away into an angry rumble, Noel was saying something about rain, and how everything needed a good drenching.

"Never mind the rain." Sheila clenched her hands. "Noel, if you won't do this for my sake, do it for yours. We have to give Matt to the law. We have to tell the police what happened. Even if you go to jail for helping me cover up Vanessa's murder, wouldn't that be better than having Aubrey's blood on your hands? Or even Matt's? Your own brother's blood?"

Noel grabbed her wrist with his left hand. He wasn't laughing

211

now. He wasn't fond. "You stupid fool, don't you get it even now? I already have blood on my hands!"

"I know. Jack. But don't worry, I'll swear I killed—"

"Not just Jack. Vanessa. Matt didn't kill her. I did."

Chapter 32

THUNDER MUTTERED in the abrupt stillness. Sheila was robbed of words and could only stare, shaking her head. Matt said softly: "I thought so." Aubrey wriggled back against the wall.

"But," Sheila faltered, "you always told me.... Why?"

"Why? Can't you guess? It was his fault — again." Noel stabbed the gun at Matt. "I brought her to the island that summer, and right away he was at her, trying to get her back."

Matt laughed. "You idiot!"

"Shut it! You *were*. See, dear, you didn't know, but I was watching them and I knew. He was meeting her secretly. So one day I followed them up to the cottage and I watched them arguing. And then after he went away I came out and I told her we had to talk. I needed to know the truth. She, she said things. About me. About him. *Comparing*." Noel choked and caught his breath. "I was angry and she — she laughed at me. Laughed! And then she turned her back and walked away."

He stood a moment breathing. Then said quietly, "She shouldn't have laughed."

"What happened?" Sheila faltered. "H-how...."

"Not much to tell." He shrugged one shoulder. "I didn't think, I just picked up a stone, one of the ones that fell from the chimney, and I hit her. Smashed her skull."

They were all staring at him. He smiled around. "So now you know. And yes, Sheila, I was lying to you, saying I saw Matt do this or that. I'm a much better liar than you are. You're really bad at it, aren't you? That's why I can't have you sacrificing yourself, telling things to the police, because sooner or later they'll trip you up and get the truth out of you. No, we have no choice. We have to get rid of those two and it has to be watertight and foolproof."

Sheila looked as if she'd been hit by a truck and just hadn't fallen down yet. Aubrey was murmuring at her. Matt was watching Noel.

Noel went to the doorway again and glanced out sideways. "There now, the boats are all gone. Listen to that thunder! Well, we don't want the storm to catch us, so I believe the moment has come." He stepped toward Aubrey, who had worked himself to a sitting position against the wall. "Keep still. I'll make this quick and tidy." He pointed the gun and steadied his right hand with his left. He took aim. "You won't feel—"

A crash like cannon fire exploded directly overhead. The air inside the cottage crackled and flashed blue. Noel froze. Sheila threw herself at him screaming.

Noel recovered almost instantly. He elbowed Sheila away. She fell against the wall, her head striking with a thwack, and slid down. "Sorry, dear, sorry, but you mustn't—" Noel waved the gun apologetically. Aubrey leaned awkwardly over her. Matt was up on his knees, levering himself up the wall, then on his feet, and in the midst of struggling he met Cally's eyes and jerked his head, signalling *Get out of here!*

"Now you." Noel levelled the gun at him. "You I will shoot with pleasure. You—"

Cally scooped up the stone from beside her foot and heaved it with all her strength through the window. It missed Noel by a foot, but he swung toward it. "Noel!" she shouted. "Out here!"

Then she ran. In two seconds she was at the cliff edge and then she was slithering over, catching at the rocks, tearing her hands. She fetched up in the hollow of the left eye, her fingers jammed into a crevice, her feet braced on a jutting cheekbone.

"Cally!" Noel's voice a dozen feet above. "Cally, are you all right?"

You'd swear he cares. Maybe he does.

But he still has that gun.

She kept still and silent.

"Cally, I can't see you! How far down are you?"

She clung to the rock like a snail.

What was that smoke smell? Wait: the lightning, that crack, the blue flash. The cottage had been struck. The cottage was burning. With Matt and Aubrey bound and helpless, and Sheila maybe concussed, unconscious.

Got to get up there. Got to get up there now!

"Cally? Cally, sit tight! I'm coming down!"

A grating, sliding sound came from above, then a pair of feet in tan leather wingtips, and then Noel was balanced on the curve of the cheekbone, left hand flung out for balance, right hand groping. For a moment he teetered, one smooth-soled shoe sliding, and Cally's mind floated in limbo.

Thinking: one good push and that would be that. Exit Noel. Nobody else would have to die.

Then: *No.* She grabbed his left hand and pulled him in.

He collapsed against the rock face, gasping. "Oh Cally, thank you! For a moment there I thought I'd had it." He smiled at her over his arm, and it was the warm, sweet, dryly humorous Noel she once thought she knew. "You saved my life. Darling Cally."

They clung to the rock almost side by side, less than an arm's reach between them. Cally glanced down past her feet. From here she could only see rocks going down and down, and then emptiness, and water far below. Lightning flashed and the water flared blue-silver.

"The cottage is on fire. Are they all out of there?"

"Not when I last looked." He smiled again, pleased, confidential. "I hadn't planned for that, but it does solve everything quite neatly."

"But — how can you — what about Sheila?"

He grimaced, pained. "I love Sheila. But you know, she was becoming a hazard. Unreliable." Then he looked at her. "Like you, Cally. I do so wish you'd stayed in the house! How did you get out, by the way?"

"Jack had tools. I took the pins out of the hinges on the door."

"Easy as that!" He laughed. "You're so clever. I wish, oh, how I wish — but it's no good." Shaking his head, smiling, he reached over, grabbed her wrist and yanked.

Chapter 33

SOMEONE ONCE told Cally, possibly intending to be funny, that the prospect of being killed in the next sixty seconds has a wonderful way of focusing your mind.

Her mind was so focused that time slowed and matter was magnified. Her sideways lurch carried her past the bulge of the giant cheekbone. Her hands drifted to its surface and flattened. Stone poured past, quartz crystals in the granite twinkling in the lightning flashes. Stone scoured her palms and bit her knees and fingertips.

A high sound hung in the air around her: someone screaming. Her sneaker toes slid into a crevice and stuck, and for a moment she was in danger of flipping over and hanging by her toes, after which she would certainly fall head-first to the stony beach now about one hundred and sixty feet below.

Don't want that to happen.

Her toes pulled out and slid on downward. Her fingers clung like octopus tentacles. The downward slide was diagonal now, funnelling her into a channel between a long mass of rock to her left — the giant's nose — and the rough undercut plane below the cheekbone.

Wish that idiot would stop screaming.

Hands and toes clawed at the channel. Slowing her. Drifting her down like ash, like the specks of ash drifting down with her.

Ash. The cottage was burning. Matt — Sheila —

Something wrong with her hands. Her toes. Something flapped about her feet. Slowing, drifting—

Stopped. So hard and sudden, as if the cliff had hammered her.

217

She wasn't sliding any more. She wasn't drifting. She was lying on the out-jutting upper lip, arms and legs all out like starfish, fingertips clamped.

Thank God the screaming's stopped.

The upper lip. Wasn't this where Ginevra fetched up, that time she fell?

Lucky I fell face-inward, not on my back. Or I might have hurt something, like Gin.

High above, something went *crack*. Not thunder, not stone on stone.

And again. *Crack* and right away a second *crack*, a different sound, and slivers of stone sprang off the giant's lip about six inches beyond her right hand. She pulled her hand back, stared wonderingly at the five red marks on the stone, stared at the broken spot. Then looked up. Noel was up there, looking weirdly foreshortened, like a character in a cartoon. He braced his feet against the giant's cheek-bone and steadied his right hand with his left.

Cally crushed herself back against the rock. Stone splintered again, this time to her left.

Can't stay here.

But there's nowhere to go.

There was, there was a bottom lip. And between the lips a hollow, a hiding place. *Go!*

She scrambled over the edge, clinging with her sticky hands, flailing with her strange-feeling bare toes. Air, nothing else.

But there was a bottom lip, there had to be, just under there. And a safe little hollow. Unless she missed it and fell. If she fell there was no place to go but down, fifty feet or so in free fall, past the receding jaw to the boulders on the beach. And full stop.

Focus.

She gripped the stone lip with both hands. *Crack* went the stone again beside them. Sharp bits flew in her face. She shut her eyes, slithered, clung tight, swung inward. She fell into the giant's mouth and lay there like a crumb to be pecked off by the birds.

SHE GUESSED LATER that she lost her focus completely at that point, because all she saw was the lake, black frilled with white, and all she heard was thunder, sounding like chests of drawers tumbling downstairs. The cry above might have been a gull's scream. The small black thing that fell past her in a long arc might have been just another rock.

After that there was nothing until.... "Cally!" Someone shook her roughly. "Oh God, your hands! Your feet!"

Matt. "You're alive?"

He knelt beside her inside the giant's mouth. There was just room for them both. "And so are the others, before you ask. But we need to get you down. The cottage is about to collapse."

"How did you get down here?" She tried to sit up, but her arms and legs belonged to someone else. They wouldn't obey her. "He shot you!"

"Just grazed me." He held up a loop of rope. "This has been stored in the cottage since the year Gin fell. Just in case."

More of the rope swung up the cliff behind him. "Who's holding that?"

"Nobody. It's anchored around one of those timber supports in the cottage. Which is *burning*. Which is why we have to get off here now!" He slipped an arm under her and propped her up.

The rope wasn't a ladder, just a thick cable with big knots in it. "I'll never get down that!"

"I know. So you and I, Cally, we're going to get really close."

That was how she came to be floating with her arms around Matt's neck, his face in her hair and her legs wrapped around his waist. She had to admit (strictly to herself) that she had dreamed of something like this, but the dreams had never involved dangling in mid-air with people yelling at her from below. Nor a sky above full of fire, and fragments of flaming debris lashing down all around.

When they reached the beach the red boat was there, floating a few feet out. Noel sat in the back seat staring at nothing. Aubrey sat in the front seat holding his head. Sheila, who had been shouting, guided them down to the beach and untied them. Matt carried Cally to the boat and plunked her in beside Noel, who did not notice. Then they were all in, crowding together, and Sheila powered up and took them away from there with a roar.

Matt, who sat on Cally's other side and kept his arm wrapped around her shoulders, said something about checking the house. Cally thought at first he meant the cottage, but when she looked up it was a mass of burning timbers and blackening stones. Orange flames danced in the meadow of dry grass and down the scrubby hillside south of the cliff.

Sheila drove the boat farther out to avoid the flying ash and sparks, then headed eastward, paralleling the south shore.

Now the whole forest was on fire. Billows of black-speckled smoke mushroomed into the sky, punctured by bursts of burning pine needles. Saplings sprang alight all at once, like giant candles. Bigger trees exploded like bombs. Even down on the water the air was hot and smelled of boiling resin. The voice of the fire was a roar that drowned out the thunder.

"Gin!" Cally said with a gasp, and felt she had just wakened from a stupor. "Where—"

"Safe." Matt squeezed her shoulder.

"How," Aubrey began, then laughed. "I get it. Mrs. Gardner?"

"Right. We arranged it between us yesterday."

After Noel found out she could walk. And might have seen something. Cally turned her head carefully to look at Noel, but he was lost somewhere far away.

She looked back at Matt. "Make like a bunny and hop it?"

He grinned. "Yep, that was the signal for Gin to go to a spot we'd chosen on the north shore. There's a hiding place there on the beach, under a windfall tree. She was to go there as soon as possible and wait for Mrs. G to come pick her up in the outboard."

With an effort Sheila said: "I'm sorry. I was so wrong. So wrong about everything."

"Not your fault," Matt said.

When they rounded the southeast headland it seemed at first that they might land safely here. The pier and the nearby trees were untouched. The house sparkled clean and white, surrounded by its moist green lawns.

But the forest was blazing at the edge of the velvet grass, and shreds of flaming debris blew on the hot west wind toward the house.

"We can't stay here," Matt said. "We'll have to try for Blackwater Bay." He looked up at the churning sky. "And pray we don't get struck by lightning on the way over." The clouds ripped open as he spoke. The flash dazzled their eyes.

Sheila turned the boat southwest. When Cally looked back, the island was a sky-high bonfire striping the dark water with the colors of blood and sunset.

Chapter 34

"THEN THE DELUGE started," Cally told Ginevra hours later. "The boat filled with water almost as fast as we could bail! For a while I was afraid we weren't going to make it."

"But we did make it," Aubrey put in. "And the rain's put out the fire, so they say. All in all we've been amazingly lucky!" He gazed with bleary-eyed satisfaction around the crowded hospital room. Its windows overlooked Port Devon's marina, where the boats rocked and the wharfs glistened silver in the wind-whipped rain.

It was Aubrey's room, and he was propped up in bed. Of them all he was the worst injured: a skull fracture. Matt's bullet wound was superficial, and bled more than it hurt, he said.

Cally's wounds had made even the doctor wince when she saw them. Her hands, knees and toes looked like raw meat. She hadn't lost as much skin as they first feared, but most of her useful parts were now heavily bandaged. She wondered how she would eat, dress, or go to the bathroom.

Sheila had only bruised the back of her head. She'd mimed unconsciousness until Noel had left the cottage in pursuit of Cally. Then she'd shot to her feet, found a utility knife, and cut Matt and Aubrey free. Matt had gone after Noel. Sheila had led Aubrey out, swaying, and gone looking for Noel's boat. There was no question of staying in the cottage, which was already burning.

Even Noel had to be patched up. One finger was taped where a thrown rock had broken a bone: the rock that Matt threw to knock the gun from his hand. Matt had feared that Noel might jump then, knowing he'd lost this game he'd created. But he simply climbed back up and followed Aubrey and Sheila down to the boat by the hill path. He had not said a word then or since.

Sheila was not with them now. She was with Noel at the OPP station waiting for their lawyer to arrive. Aubrey fretted, wanting to be with her, even though she had cold-shouldered him again.

"My gosh, lucky!" Gin said. She had been bouncing with excitement ever since she'd arrived with Mrs. Gardner. They'd come the long way from Blackwater Bay, by road. "Matt, you'd be dead now if Cally didn't throw that stone!"

"That wasn't luck." Matt tugged one of her tumbled curls. "That was all Cally. The one stroke of real luck in this whole mess was Sheila spotting Noel when he circled back in the boat."

"But that was a lucky throw, right, when you knocked the gun out of Noel's hand?"

"Of course not. That was skill."

"You're a hero!" She grabbed his hand and swung it.

"And you are a little donkey. Didn't I tell you not to go roaming at night? What the hell did you think you were doing?"

"Don't nag! I couldn't resist. I hate being left out of things."

"You could've got left out permanently," Aubrey said. "You saw Noel that night with Jack, didn't you? Why didn't you tell somebody?"

"Because all I saw was him watching him. Noel watching Jack, I mean. It scared me. There was something about the way he, Noel, he looked." She pulled Matt's hand close and wrapped her arms around it. "So I went away. And then when he asked me about it next day, I was afraid of him. So I said I didn't see anything."

Matt had been watching her with a grim look on his face. "Well, that worked out all right. But it was awful damn close." He stood up

223

and looked at the window, where hail rattled. "I hope the house is safe. We can't go back there for a while yet, though. And Gin will still need lessons."

"Lessons! You're kidding!" Gin collapsed into her chair, thunderstruck. "I thought you'd forget!"

"I never forget. Anything." Matt shot a glance at Cally. He added, "Mrs. Gardner, I'd take it as a kindness if you'd keep Gin for tonight. I'm going to the OPP station to see if Sheila and Noel need anything."

"Sheila yes, but Noel?" Aubrey opened his eyes wide. "He was all set to kill you! And me! And he would've shot Cally!"

"He's still my brother." Matt headed for the door.

"Wait." Cally got up awkwardly, because it hurt to use her hands for leverage. "Wait. I'm coming with you."

224

Chapter 35

ON THE LAST Sunday in July Cally sat on the terrace looking out over the lawn and through the trees to the glittering lake. It was her first morning on the island after having spent the past few weeks in Toronto. She wore a long white sundress to cover the ugly scabbed patches on her knees.

After two weeks of steady drizzle the island, too, was beginning to heal. The lower third was vibrantly green and full of life. The rain had scoured the house clean of soot, and nobody could have guessed, by looking at it, how close it had come to destruction.

The air was so clean and clear that Cally could see the details of boathouses on the far shore. A trick of the breeze carried the sound of church bells two miles across the water from Blackwater Bay, their clangour muted to silvery sweetness.

Behind her through an open window came the clink of cutlery and china as Edna cleared the breakfast table. She had come back after Mrs. Gardner convinced her there would be no more murders. It helped that the police had taken away Vanessa's bones, which they had found jumbled in a charred blanket under a mass of burned cedar boughs halfway down the north slope of the island.

Ginevra's laughter rang up from the beach, and Aubrey's with it. Sheila was down there too, supervising the building of the bonfire. It was safe now to light a fire. She had made up her mind to burn all of what she called her "fear and loathing" pictures. When Cally had protested the destruction of all those wonderful pieces, Sheila said, "I can't stand to look at them and I won't sell them. Better to lighten the darkness with them."

The bonfire was set for nightfall. Ginny had insisted there had to be hot dogs and marshmallows to roast and Aubrey had brought some from the village.

Cally smiled, thinking of Aubrey. He and Sheila had come to an understanding. Nothing had yet been said aloud, but it coloured every look they sent each other, every move they made around each other. *Good for them. They should be happy, Sheila especially.*

Sheila was now in a legal limbo, which she said was not as uncomfortable as it sounded. She had been released into her older brother's custody pending her hearing. Her lawyer was confident that given the circumstances — being deceived by Noel, fear for her father's health, and the deep sense of guilt that had nearly unbalanced her mind — she would not go to prison as an accessory.

Noel had been charged with murder. He could have gotten bail, but decided to stay in jail. He would speak only to Sheila and his lawyer. Cally thought of him with an ache at the heart, but she couldn't wish him free. Not yet.

Of course he had lost custody of Ginevra, who was now Matt's ward — to Gin's extravagant delight. Matt had decided not to send her to boarding school, but to keep her with him. "She needs a normal family life, that kid. Needs to be civilized — if that's ever possible. I still don't know how two lambs like Dad and Francesca produced a little tiger like Gin!"

THE FRONT DOOR opened and closed. Measured, quiet footsteps sounded on the flagstones. Cally marvelled at how lightly he could move, given his size. And how she knew his step now.

But she would have known he was there even without the sound of footsteps. When he stopped behind her chair she lifted her head

226

and inhaled. His aftershave, and the smell of coffee and bacon, and something else that was warm and spicy and all his own — the scent of his skin.

Something was missing. She sniffed again. "You've given up smoking?"

"Yep, finally. This time for good. I hope." He pulled up a chair beside hers. "I want to thank you for spending so much time with Gin in town, these past weeks," he said in a formal tone. "You and Aubrey both. And Mrs. G, of course. Gin needs familiar faces after all she's been through."

"I was happy to." *Yet I hardly saw anything of you.*

"And thanks for joining us on the island again. Seems it's not finished with us yet. How are your wounds?"

She held out her hands to show the shiny red skin on the fingertips and knuckles where the abrasions were still in a midway stage of healing. "Tender, but soon as good as new."

Ginevra's high, excited voice carried through the trees. Matt laughed softly. Cally said, "Everybody loves a bonfire. All the cleansing power of a forest fire and none of the terror."

"Cleansing?"

"The past. I think Sheila may really be ready to move on from here."

"I hope to God that's true," he said quietly. Then added, "But I'm not burning my thousand-dollar picture!"

"Good investment?"

"Memory." His voice darkened. "It's not my way to wipe out the past completely. I need to learn to live with it. At least some of it."

He abandoned the flimsy chair and stood at the edge of the terrace. The emerald lawn still glittered with dew in the shadow of the house. The breeze brought the smell of soaked, burned wood and earth, mingling uneasily with the sweetness of alyssum.

He looked back at her. "Will you walk with me? Talking's easier when I'm walking."

They crossed the emerald lawn and started up the path through the blackened woods. The stone-dust path was strewn with debris that crunched under Cally's sandal soles. The stink of burning rose around them and the spikes of charred trees were everywhere. It was like walking through the ruins of a bombed-out cathedral.

Still silent, they left the burned woods and crossed the meadow, an expanse of caked, cracking charcoal. The ground felt unnervingly warm through the soles of her shoes. You could imagine that the embers still glowed, deep down.

Matt whistled as they approached the cottage. They walked in a circle around it. The walls had collapsed. The stones, so deeply fire-scarred that even the rain hadn't washed them clean, gaped at the sky like a mouthful of broken teeth. "A total loss! And I thought it would last forever."

"I'm glad it's destroyed," Cally said passionately. "It was a bad place and it did a lot of harm. No, don't laugh! It drew violence like a magnet. It should have been knocked down years ago." A thought struck her and she laid an urgent hand on his arm. "You're not planning to rebuild it!"

"No, I'll just leave it. With time it will go back to the earth and the woods, where it came from. Besides, we — Noel and I — we'll be selling out. This island is one part of the past I want to put behind me, and he feels the same."

"I'm glad you've been talking, even if it's only through Sheila. Do you think you could ever be friends?" She looked up at him hopefully. He shook his head.

"I'm afraid that's too much to ask. Maybe if I'd been able to see what he was feeling back when we were kids. When Julia died, perhaps. Maybe if I'd reached out then. But I didn't. And after that it was too late."

"How old were you then? Eleven or twelve? How could you have known?"

"All the same, it should never have come to this." He turned his back on the cottage and they walked side by side across the burned meadow to the cliff edge.

Cally hung back but Matt stepped to the brink and looked down past his feet. He said: "I'll never be able to look at Noel again without remembering how he tried to kill you on the cliff down there. And how he killed Vanessa and Jack. And you remember Gin always swore she was pushed, that time she fell? Well, she was. That was Noel too."

"What? No!"

He turned to face her. "Yes. He confessed it to Sheila, and she told me. Well, you know what Gin's like. She was just the same at seven, especially when she was bored and had nobody to play with: snooping around, looking for mischief." He grinned; then his mouth tightened. "And she was always up at the cottage, sometimes alone. Noel was afraid she'd nose out something about Vanessa."

"I can't believe even Noel would do that!"

"I wish it wasn't true. But it is. And it's come out that he was also behind most of the vandalism on the island this summer. He sabotaged the canoe, for one thing. And he was the mystery man who knocked you out in the woods."

"All to make you look bad?"

"That was only part of it. I could've been forced to stop work on the cottage. Maybe to sell out to Noel."

"So that's why he kept asking you—"

229

"Right. If he'd owned my part of the island, he could have made sure Vanessa's secret would stay secret. But with me messing about there, any day those bones could have come to light." He slanted a smile at her. "Funny how it took you and Aubrey, the two outsiders."

They were silent a long moment. Cally took a step and looked down the cliff face. Gin would have been standing just about here, above the nose.

"And on his side," Matt went on, "I don't think Noel will ever be able to give up hating me. I think he's become addicted to hatred. It gives him a sense of purpose. And I guess it's easier to hate me than admit he's been wrong."

"Not Sheila, though."

"No." His tight mouth softened. "I can thank you, Cally, for giving me back my sister." His hand closed around hers and held on.

The waterscape was a sweep of sapphire and aquamarine under the clean arch of the sky. Cally glanced sideways at Matt and saw that his eyes had caught some of that rich color. And he was looking at her.

"It can be so beautiful here," she said, with a suddenly shortened breath.

"It can. So, take a look around. Say goodbye. We won't be coming back to this place. Ever been to Nova Scotia?"

The change of subject jolted her. "Nova Scotia! No, never."

"We'll be moving there."

"Who, uh, who's 'we'?"

"Gin and I. Maybe Sheila too, for a while. And Mrs. G if I can persuade her to uproot herself from Ontario."

Something pinched inside Cally's chest. "Why?"

"My firm is opening a branch in Halifax. We're doing well, we're expanding. I'll be the principal there."

"Congratulations! That's wonderful!" The pinched place hurt a little more.

"Beautiful place, Nova Scotia. Lots of great little towns along the Atlantic coast." He planted his feet, still right on the brink, and clinked the keys in his pocket. "I've had my eye on a property within commuting distance of Halifax. Thinking I'll design and build a house there, within sight and sound of the sea. A place to live year round, not just in summer. What do you think?" His tone was studiously casual.

"Your own special house by the sea? Sounds like a dream come to life!"

"It wouldn't be as isolated as it sounds. It's just outside a village. And there aren't anywhere near as many blizzards and hurricanes as you might think."

"Oh, good."

"Could you stand living in a place like that, Cally?"

"Could I?" Her heart thumped. Her voice went deadpan. "It would depend on the company, wouldn't it?"

"Sup—" He cleared his throat. "Supposing it were me?"

A bubble of joy rose up inside her and burst free. She threw back her head and laughed aloud, couldn't help it. He took her by one arm and gently swung her around, then held her off at both arms' length to search her eyes. "All right then, that's settled," he said after a moment, and pulled her close.

There were no more words. None were needed. As they walked back past the ruin of the cottage, Cally felt the burden of years of fear and hatred blowing away like feathers of soot on the wind. The past was laid open to the cleansing sky. The ghosts were gone.

About the author

PATRICIA BOW lives in Kitchener, Ontario. She has written more than twenty books for readers of all ages who love mystery, suspense and fantasy. To find out more about Patricia and her work, visit her web page at www.execulink.com/~thebows/patricia.htm.

JACQUES BERGUR

GOEBIUS' STRANGE MODEL

ISBN: 978-2-9550219-1-0

Cover design by kouvertures.com